D1248534

A VERSION OF

ᘓ LOVE ᘔ

ALSO BY MILLICENT DILLON

FICTION

Baby Perpetua and Other Stories
The One in the Back Is Medea
The Dance of the Mothers
Harry Gold

NONFICTION

A Little Original Sin: The Life and Work of Jane Bowles
After Egypt: Isadora Duncan and Mary Cassatt
You Are Not I: A Portrait of Paul Bowles
Out in the World: The Selected Letters of Jane Bowles (editor)
The Viking Portable Paul and Jane Bowles (editor)

A VERSION OF

∽ LOVE ∽

Millicent Dillon

W. W. NORTON & COMPANY

NEW YORK • LONDON

For information about permission to reproduce selections from this book,
write to Permissions, W. W. Norton & Company, Inc., 500 Fifth Avenue,
New York, NY 10110

Manufacturing by the Haddon Craftsmen, Inc.
Book design by BTDnyc
Production manager: Julia Druskin

Library of Congress Cataloging-in-Publication Data

Dillon, Millicent.
A version of love / Millicent Dillon.—1st ed.
p. cm.
ISBN 0-393-05216-8 (hardcover)
1. Triangles (Interpersonal relations)—Fiction. 2. Psychotherapist and patient—
Fiction. 3. Hysteria—Patients—Fiction. 4. Gold mines and mining—Fiction.
5. California—Fiction. 6. Mexico—Fiction. I. Title.

PS3554.I43 V47 2003
813'.54—dc21   2002152906

W. W. Norton & Company, Inc., 500 Fifth Avenue, New York, N.Y. 10110
www.wwnorton.com

W. W. Norton & Company Ltd., Castle House, 75/76 Wells Street, London
W1T 3QT

1 2 3 4 5 6 7 8 9 0

To Joan Smith and Freda Birnbaum

A VERSION OF
ᴄ⁓ LOVE ⁓ᴐ

CHAPTER

~ I ~

A MAN AND A WOMAN ARE DRIVING ON A COUNTRY ROAD IN
the late afternoon heat. On either side of them are dry meadows
flanked by tawny hills. As the top of the car is down, their words drift
backward in the onrush of air.

"What was that burning mound?"

". . . tailings . . . waste left by miners."

"So they still . . ."

"Here and there . . . a few . . ."

He does not call her by name but, after all, in ordinary conversation
it is not necessary to address the other as John, Mary, Fred, whoever,
before you say what you have to say, if only two of you are there.

She does not call him by name, either. She looks at his hands as
they grasp the wheel. She says to herself: I am here with him. He and
I are on this road, together.

Yet between them are sudden distances and long slow lapses. Though there are only a few inches separating his body from hers, between them are borders to be crossed and recrossed, a no-man's-no-woman's-land where an inch, a foot, a mile has no meaning.

The distant hills have moved in closer. The road has begun to wind more tightly. In the slanting sunlight the car leans into each oncoming curve.

They are being sped along by risk, which is expanding each moment, calling all else—everything that is not risk—into question.

CHAPTER

2

IT WAS LIKE ANY AUTO CAMP OF THE TIME—1959 OR 1960:
a rustic compound of wooden cabins clustered in a barren space
surrounded by trees. Above the small office was a red electric sign,
"Vacanc ," with the "y" missing.

She waited outside in the dark while he went in. She could see
him talking to the proprietor, a gray-haired man with a bony face,
wearing a red plaid shirt and a tan cardigan. She saw him register,
she saw him hand over cash, she did not see how much. Not that it
mattered—

She looked up into the night sky. The moon had not yet risen.
So many stars, a vault of stars. . . . Such vastness was enough to
set her adrift. She turned and saw him standing in the doorway of
the office, a dark form silhouetted against the light, and she was
reassured.

Inside the cabin the first thing she noticed was the smell of mold. Then she saw a bed with a green bedspread, an overhead light, muddy brown wall paneling edged by shiny green strips, and two wooden chairs at a scratched wooden table. In the small bathroom: a toilet, a sink and a shower with a grimy plastic curtain, the smell from that, she guessed.

He stood at the center of the room, looking around. "Are you hungry?" he asked abruptly.

She wasn't. "Yes, I could eat something."

He went out to the car and came back in with the ice chest. He took out a package wrapped in wax paper, unwrapped it, laid out sandwiches, and poured coffee from a thermos into two cups. From his bag he pulled out a flask of whiskey and asked if she wanted some in her coffee. She shook her head no. He poured some into his, and put the flask in front of him.

It was the first time they had shared a meal.

"The lamb is very good," she said.

"Leftovers. It's always better the next day."

He poured himself another cup of coffee, and put more whiskey in it.

"You've been here before?" she asked.

"You mean this motel?"

"No, I mean this area." She gestured outside.

"Many times."

She could have asked When? With whom? But she did not. A hole had been left open. There would be many more holes to come, holes not to fall into, to keep each other out of.

He said that he loved to drive, loved just getting into the car and going. "When I was a kid, I used to drive for days without stopping."

"Was that safe?"

"I've never had an accident."

Tempting words, she thought, to provoke Chance, Fate, whatever. Surreptitiously she knocked on the table.

"Are you done?" he asked.

"Yes, I'm done."

He stood and started to clean up.

"I'll do it," she said.

"It's nothing."

He cleared the table except for the coffee and whiskey. He poured more whiskey into his cup. He looked around the room. "Not a great place," he said, "is it? Well, it's only for the night."

He got up and went to his bag, pulled out a map and came back to sit at the table across from her. He placed the map on the scarred surface and examined it in the light of the overhead bulb. "We're near here," he pointed to a large shaded area. "We'll follow this road north tomorrow." His index finger followed a snaking line.

She followed his gesture upside down. She tried to visualize a road, not a line, but she saw only his finger on the flat plane.

He folded the map and got up and went to his bag again. With his back to her, she warned herself against watching his every move so intently it bordered on surveillance. But it wasn't spying. It was simply the amazement of being here with him that made her want to look and look at him again, to prove that it was so.

She made herself get up and go to her bag and open it and pull out the small case with her toilet articles. In the bathroom she turned on the light. The smell of the mold was even stronger here. She sniffed at the shower curtain. Yes, that was the source of the odor. She looked about for a window to open to air things out. There was no window in here.

Above the toilet was a narrow shelf. Setting the case on it, she turned and looked into the mirror above the sink. The glass was crazed around the edges but from the mirror's center her image was clearly reflected back to her. She was surprised at how calm she looked, even though her pulse had become rapid.

Once this would have been a warning that it was time to hold the pressure of excitement in check, not to let it build to the point where it could consume you from the inside out, like fire, like an explosion. But now it only served to spur her on: the more excitement, the further she would go. It was, perhaps, a test of how far she could go.

When she went back into the room, she found him seated at the table once more, a book in front of him. "What are you reading?"

"It's a guidebook of the area. It's got some interesting information about mining. Maybe you'd like to hear . . . ?"

"Sure," she said. Mining couldn't have been further from her mind.

He read about how at first the gold lay around just for the taking. He read that the earliest mines were all placer mines, involving extracting loose bits of gold from the intermixed sand, gravel and boulders in a streambed or hillside. He read about the technique individual miners used, sifting the streambeds over and over, pebble by pebble.

"But by 1852 those deposits were all but exhausted. And now mining companies began to use hydraulic extraction. With water under enormous pressure every square inch of rock was blasted, every square foot of dirt crushed and screened and washed and searched again. . . . Hillsides were flooded, orchards uprooted, houses undermined. . . ."

She was only half listening to his words. She was extracting desire out of the words, out of his voice uttering the words. The words themselves had nothing to do with desire, yet how was it, they were becoming the ally, the further incitement of desire.

SHE AWOKE FROM A DREAM THAT SHE WAS IN A ROOM WITH him to find she was in a room with him.

There was sunlight on the window shade. The brown of the paneling was no longer muddy, the green less shiny, the smell of mold fainter. He was sleeping, turned away from her.

She had barely slept. For hours she lay awake, suspended in a state of thinking, not thinking, believing, disbelieving, the sex she had been through with him still streaming within her. But now in the morning light, the moment she tried to grasp that actuality—each motion, each sensation—it kept slipping away, as if it had been dispersed, drop by drop, into every cell of her body.

He turned toward her and opened his eyes, and she saw in the way he looked at her that he was surprised. Surprised that it was she—and not another?

No, she was not going to go down that path, of jealousy and even worse cruelties.

"Why are you shaking your head?"

"No reason."

He got up and raised the blind. She saw slanted sunlight streaming through the trees. He turned from the window and walked to the bathroom. In her mind, in her vision of him, two images alternated, one replacing the other, then it in turn being replaced. The first, a strong steady body, a shining secret body. And the second, a heavy torso, a soft belly, a flaccid penis. Two images fighting for place in this room, and the room changing with the image as well, a shining image, a shining room, a dull flat image, a dull flat room.

She heard the sound of the toilet flushing. She heard the water running in the shower. The shower was turned off, and soon after she heard the hum of the electric razor.

She sat up. She saw the book upon the table. In the wake of competing images, she felt the rush of unappeasable desire. Was that the nature of all desire, or just of her desire for him, unappeasable in the sense that it was always being notched up yet one more level?

And his desire for her? She thought of his eyes as he awoke. Perhaps he was only caught in a dream at that moment. Good God, you can't hold him accountable for his dream. (Yes but meaning, yes but wish . . .)

The humming stopped.

In the silence she reassured herself, This is what he does every morning: he pees, he showers, he shaves.

And maybe he always wakes up surprised.

4

THE AIR IN THE ROADSIDE DINER WAS SATURATED WITH THE smell of bacon frying, of coffee brewing, of cigarette smoke. As they slid into one of the red plastic booths, several burly men at the counter turned and looked at them. It came to her that this was the first time he and she had been seen together by others.

These men know nothing of him or of her. Yet, from a slight shift in his posture, from something in his eyes that was like a willed deflection, she had the sense that he thought that they could know.

She wanted to say, What does it matter if they know or don't know? But she didn't.

The waitress appeared to take their order, and when she went away, he picked up a newspaper that had been left in the booth. He scanned the headlines and asked, "Do you want to see what's going on in the outside world?"

"No, thanks." Today, just for today, she wanted to stay in this world, whatever it was, this one she was in with him.

The waitress brought orange juice and coffee, and he put the paper aside. After he drank the coffee, he lit a cigarette and smiled at her.

"Good coffee."

Taking the guidebook from his jacket pocket, he set it before him on the table. "There's a note in here about an old mine shaft. It's real close."

She watched as he leafed through the pages. Once again, as if on signal, she was flooded with desire. A little like Pavlov's dog, she realized.

"Do you remember that dog howling outside the window last night?"

"No, I don't remember." He stubbed out his cigarette. "Why do you ask?"

"No reason."

"Was there something special about it?"

"No, it was only a howling dog."

He shrugged and let it pass.

On their way out, he stopped to pay the cashier. Watching—now she was watching him with another—she saw the way the young woman looked at him. She saw the admiration—the desire—in her gaze. Why did she think of Pavlov's dog again? Dogs don't look through others' eyes. Yet here she was, right on signal, seeing him as the woman was seeing him: a striking man with deep blue eyes, and a powerful, even commanding presence. Another's eyes confirming for her that to be with a man of such qualities was surely to have been chosen.

They were driving north. The morning air was pleasantly cool. There was very little traffic. Now and then they passed a car coming in the opposite direction, the driver little more than a vague before, a blur, no after.

On either side of the road, beyond the fields of dry grass, hills rose and fell. Where the base of one hill sloped into another, there was a hollow of shade, an outcropping of a surprisingly deep green.

"What was with the dog?" he asked.

"The dog last night? It was loud."

"It kept you up?"

"Yes."

"I slept like a stone."

"Actually, well, actually, you didn't sleep through it."

"No?"

"You'd half wake up and swear at the noise, and then fall back to sleep, and wake up and swear, and finally, you leaned over and opened the window and started howling yourself."

"Did I? And what happened?"

"The dog stopped."

"Oh?" He laughed. A slightly embarrassed, even an uneasy laugh. "Well, at least it worked. It shut him up."

"It did do that."

"On that hill over there," he said, "do you see that headframe?"

So, once again, gold mining was to be their subject.

"What is it?"

"It's a scaffold. It marks the shaft of a hard-rock mine."

"The one you mentioned?"

"No, that one is farther on."

He spoke of riffles, of toms, of other things she did not quite catch, and then, still looking at the road ahead, he said, "Did I growl and bare my teeth?"

"No, you just howled."

In the silence she wondered why he said what he said about teeth, but then she decided it was not necessary to take his every word and hold it as hostage to meaning. Perhaps she should not have told him about the dog, after all.

Up ahead and to the side was a slope with a huge gouge in it, like a raw wound.

"Is that from the mining?" she asked.

"No doubt."

"So after they ravaged this place, they just abandoned it—"

"Yes. It wasn't the first time, and it won't be the last. It's what human beings do."

Hearing the darkness in his tone—though, in profile, his face seemed impassive—she felt a chill of apprehension. She felt there was something she wanted to say in response, a thought as yet only dimly perceived, about place, about the way events invade a landscape and are never rooted out, as in the mind there are certain memories that are unaltered and unalterable, no matter what happens afterward, even if you tell about them, even if later events contradict them.

But she felt inadequate to the task, as if the only history she could speak of at the moment was their shared history—the history that had led to her being here with him.

She repeated the words to herself.

Here with him.

So suddenly and powerfully did the realization come, it was like a revelation, a belief after disbelief.

Then what was going on at this moment, at each successive moment of this trip, demanded to be realized again and again. Was that so? Did this desire, this love—yes, call it that—nurture a hidden element of desperation?

He slowed as they came to a junction; one road led off to the right, the other to the left. "That one," he said, pointing to the left, "goes to the abandoned mine shaft."

"You've been there before?"

"No." He smiled. He seemed better—more relaxed in a way. She did not know what worse had been. She did not feel she could ask him. Certain privacies of his must not be violated. And she, had she any privacies from him, after so much telling?

He made a left turn.

CHAPTER

5

SOON THE ROAD NARROWED. IT WAS BORDERED ON EITHER side by high tangled growth, hemming them in. Driving on this road with him, even as it increased the distance from where they had been, was like erasing. Not to go back, only forward.

The choice has been made, this road and not the other. Just as an earlier choice had been made. Not to go to Mexico. To come here instead. He had suggested Mexico first. She said, No, not Mexico. Mexico was too far away, too large an unknown for her, with all the other unknowns she foresaw on this trip.

So they came here instead, to a nearer, easier place. But perhaps no place is easy, harboring as all places do remnants and reminders. She looked at the road ahead, straight and narrow, like a corridor diminishing to infinity, but of course it was no such thing, simply a road to a mine shaft.

She knew, or thought she knew this much about herself, that she was driven to go in pursuit of a thought, not any thought, but a particular kind of thought (like that about the corridor) that would begin to abstract itself from reality, in search of a larger statement, a larger meaning, but soon in its convolutions it would wind tighter and tighter, and she would be caught, bound, until the moment when thought turned against itself in a sudden spasm. And then she would seize upon the visible with relief, an appropriation of the real, the outside world, outside but now somehow within.

A small dullness entered her head, a warning sign like a fear not fully formed, raw the way anxiety is raw, but only the shadow of anxiety—not real anxiety. Real anxiety takes you over—this was not taking her over.

Say that she arrives with him at the abandoned mine shaft, that she comes to the edge of it and looks down into its depths, deep in the earth, and there on that edge imagines herself falling, believing it, yet only believing it as if it were so . . . able to imagine a possibility without fearing that imagination itself can destroy you for just imagining. . . .

She heard a sound, or rather the stopping of a sound.

The car rolled to a stop. He turned the key in the ignition and started the engine again; the starter ignited but the engine did not turn over.

"Are you out of gas?"

"No, no, the tank's half full."

He tried again. Still the engine didn't catch.

"Is it flooded?"

"No, of course not, the engine can't flood as you're driving."

He got out of the car and opened the hood. "I think it's a leak in the fuel pump. If I have some tape, I may be able to fix it so it will hold until we can get to a service station."

He came back and opened the glove compartment. "Damn it, no tape."

Once more he tried to start the car. Again only the starter turned. Once more he got out of the car and looked at the engine.

By now the sun was directly overhead. She noticed the thick layering of gray dust on the leaves of the dense growth beside the road. She recalled what he said about driving, that he loved to drive, that he had never had an accident. This was no accident, it was only the dying of an engine.

"Jesus." He searched the road for the sign of another car. "Nobody." He looked at his watch. "Maybe we'd better start walking—" Yet he did not move.

She detected in herself an imperative to placate, to reassure, to pacify, to alleviate, a form of rescue, rescue by telling. Once, when she was in school, she told him, she was on a biking trip with some classmates and a tire blew out on one of the girls' bikes. Nobody had a patch kit, but one of the boys came up with a solution, only he wouldn't let the girls see what he was doing.

"Later we found out he fixed it with a rubber and some glue, but he didn't want any of the girls knowing that he had brought a rubber with him, so they . . ."

Even as she faltered, she saw he was not listening.

He was looking under the hood again, pulling on wires, testing to see if they were loose. "Last week I thought I heard a funny sound in the engine but then I didn't hear it again, so I thought it was okay."

At that moment she was reminded of a dream from last night, of being in a room, with him and another man. It was an ordinary room except for one thing. It was a room on tracks, though it was not a train.

She would not tell him her dream. It was time to think in precise everyday terms: there is no third with us. The engine has stopped. There is a leak in the fuel pump. Maybe the gasoline vapors corroded the metal. Maybe it was simply time for it to break down, not the best time for us, but still—a mechanical problem, no more, no less.

She looked over at him, past the distance between them. She was thinking about body, about his body and hers, how in sex with him there had been for an instant an almost erasure of the distance between them, but not an actual erasure, one wouldn't want that. . . .

"Look, there's a car coming," he said.

CHAPTER

6

SHE WALKED PAST THE GOLD RUSH HOTEL, PAST A BAR, A grocery, a general store, another bar, a dry goods shop. . . .

The main street of this town was like a movie set with its wooden storefronts and its flimsy balconies never meant to bear any weight. She was like a performer, unobserved, obscure, with no assigned part, but a performer acutely aware of the moisture between her thighs and under her arms. Her own inner heat was growing to match the rising outer heat, as on another hot day, years ago, in another town when she—

No, she had had enough of having to remember the past.

It came to her that up to now the future had only existed in cautionary terms. Don't do this if it's likely to precipitate that, or that if it's likely to cause this. Just to get through today, to survive. And then having gotten through it, to prepare herself for the next day's threat. But from the moment she agreed to come here, every happening had presented itself as an invitation to force her own boldness out of hiding. It had meant placing one foot in front of another on a strange path and not looking back.

Turning off the main street, she followed a dirt road that led to a cluster of shacks. The relentless sun had bleached the wooden sidings to white. In front of the last shack a rusted black sedan crouched on blocks, its inert metal body absorbing the heat of the sun and radiating it into the surrounding air.

Up ahead a path led to a slight rise, where a grove of eucalyptus trees offered relief from the sun. Standing in their shade, she saw how the bark of the trunk was peeling, revealing an underlayer of delicate green and dun yellow.

Do you mind staying? he had asked her, as he got into the tow truck with the driver to go back to get the car. No, she said, No. Was she looking for a respite? From him? From what had been happening between them that was too intense to absorb, no less comprehend? Like taking a breather before starting out again. But this was no mountain she was scaling, there was no summit to be reached.

Descending on the other side of the grove, she came to a wooden house, askew on its foundation. A fat man was sitting on a chair beside an open door, his belly slipping to either side as he slumped in the chair, a hat over his face. Above the door, "Museum" was handpainted in ornate letters.

At her approach the man took his hat from his face and opened his eyes. They were little eyes, merry in his puddinglike face, as moon-shaped as a cartoon figure.

He smiled and said, "Good day to you." His words sounded archaic, though there was nothing archaic in the way he surveyed her with his little eyes.

"A hot day to be walking around town, ain't it?"

She nodded. "Yes, very hot."

"For me the hotter it is, the better I like it." He wiggled his shoulders and grinned. "You staying at the hotel?"

"No."

"Just as well not. They charge fifteen dollars a night for a room no bigger than a closet. Just like a Gold Rush room, with Gold Rush furniture, they say. Can you believe it? Fifteen dollars? It's highway robbery, but then rich city people, tourists—"

He leaned forward.

"Why don't you step inside, little lady, and see my museum? I call it a museum, but I also sell things, all sorts of things. Of course, there are certain things I wouldn't sell no matter how much you paid me. Well, maybe, if we're talking a hundred dollars."

His right arm floated upward out of his huge body. "Go on in, see for yourself. There's no admission charge, but if you want to put a little something in my collection plate, I don't mind." He pointed to a candy jar holding a few coins on the ground beside him.

He closed his eyes, covered his face with his hat, and leaned back in the chair.

She stepped into a dark room in which the air was thick with dust. At the back a curtain, half pulled, led to an even darker room. Through the opening she saw an unmade cot and black painted walls.

She passed a table labeled "Forty-Niner Hats," then another labeled "Forty-Niner Canteens," then another labeled "Forty-Niner Shoes," with old boots, lined up in rows, two by two, their leather lamely suggesting the feet they once enclosed.

Beyond were other tables, unlabeled, piled high with things, blackened cooking pots, shot glasses, weights, boxes with weights. On a long trestle table were implements, also unlabeled, small picks and small shovels all in a heap, and off to the side a thing, curved on one end, flat on the other, part wood, part metal, the metal so filigreed by rust it resembled lace.

In the airless room she felt overwhelmed by stuff, by the disorder of things used, discarded, then reclaimed.

Stepping outside, she blinked and waited for her eyes to adjust to the intense light.

The proprietor removed the hat from his face. "So what do you think of my museum? Nice, huh?"

"It's . . . it's . . . interesting."

"Anything you got your eye on?"

"Not really." Yet out of politeness, at least she thought it politeness, she added, "I was wondering about that thing—"

"What thing? There are a lot of things in there."

"It's on the table with the tools. It's shaped like this." With her hands she described it in the air.

"Oh, that. It's called 'rocking the cradle.' Did you see the sieve at the head end of it? The miners piled the dirt they dug up on this sieve. Then they'd pour water over the dirt, and start shaking the whole thing like this"—he moved his hands back and forth vigorously, though the folds of his skin under his shirtsleeves lagged behind—"so the pieces of dirt fell through and the gold, which is a lot heavier than dirt, stayed on the top."

"It's a strange name," she said.

"Why? It looks like a cradle."

"Maybe. But you rock a baby's cradle gently to get it to sleep. They had to rock it violently—"

He laughed. "What do you expect? They were looking for gold."

"Yes, I realize that. I was just talking about the name they gave it—" she said, and started to turn away.

"So, if you want that 'rocking the cradle,' I'll give you a good price, half off. Five bucks."

"No thank you, I don't know what I'd do with it."

"You're making a mistake. Old things like that are hard to find. Someday, I can tell you this, it's going to be worth a heck of a lot of money."

She shook her head, and again turned to leave.

"Before you go. I've got something special I want to show you." He heaved his bulk out of the chair, sighing with the effort as he got to his feet. "You want to come inside and see it?"

"I should be getting along."

"Just wait one minute. I'll go inside and get it. That's all it's going to take, one minute."

In an instant—despite his bulk how fast he moved—he was back with a paper in his hands, though he was holding it so she couldn't see what was on it. He was standing so close to her, she noticed the sweat underneath his small eyes. She smelled the oddly fragrant fresh smell of his skin.

"This is the finest thing in the museum. I only show it to my special visitors." He winked and waited for her to say something, but she couldn't think of anything to say.

"It's an old letter, more than a hundred years old, written by a man named George Martin, telling what happened on the overland journey, telling all about the caravan running out of water in the desert and how thirsty they all were, they thought they were going to die of thirst. But then they came to this enormous rock, and right next to it there's this pool of water. It's like a miracle, right there in the desert. So everybody drinks and they fill their canteens, and they decide they'll rest for the night and go on the next day.

"But there's this one man—he doesn't give his name—he can't

stop drinking. He keeps drinking and drinking, though they all warn him not to. And then, that night, in the middle of the night—this thing happens."

He stopped and waited. "What happened?" she asked.

"In the middle of the night there's a terrible noise, and they all jump up and run to see what it is. It's the man who wouldn't stop drinking. He's running in a circle, and all the time he's running, he's screaming that he's going to die in that circle. They get hold of him and they tie him up. They get him quiet and they lay him down on the ground and they all go back to sleep. But in the morning when they wake up, he's gone. The rope is there, all coiled up, but he's gone."

"Where did he go?"

"They never did find him," he said, with a triumphant note in his voice. "Oh, they looked for him, all right, they looked all around the camp and out in the desert, but they never found him. So they went on. They had to go on. You can't blame them for going on. He could have been anywhere out there, running and running in circles."

Slowly he lowered himself into the chair. "It's all right there in that letter. You can see why it's the one thing in my museum I'd never sell. Never. My granddaddy got it from someone, and passed it on to me. I wouldn't sell it, not even for a hundred dollars."

He raised his eyebrows suggestively.

"Well, I thank you very much for showing it to me," she said, though he had not actually shown her the letter.

"Pleasure, ma'am. Any time." He put his hat over his face and slumped back in the chair.

She dropped fifty cents into the candy jar.

"You be careful wandering round on such a hot day," his words came through the hat.

Walking back to the main street, she told herself that when he returned with the tow truck she would tell him about the "museum." But even as she was preparing to make a joke of it, she felt a sudden irritation with the Museum Man. There was something weird in the way he told her about the letter, a kind of taunting appeal. Was it even a real letter? Or had he just made up the whole thing? But why would he do that? Still, real or not real, she could not rid herself of the image of the man running in circles, crying out. . . .

The sun beating down on her head had become unbearably hot. The light around her seemed too bright and not bright enough at the same time.

She closed her eyes. She took a deep breath. She reminded herself—roughly, not gently—of her old habits—her old illness—yes, call it that—her old symptom—to seek out darkness even, especially in the light.

Have I forgotten that I am done with that? How could I have forgotten? I am here, in this place, on this trip, with him. With him.

But still she could feel the seduction of the fat man's story, seduced once again by a story—a story of what it would be to run in ever-widening circles. . . .

You don't have to do this.

You can say, The hell with it.

I will say, The hell with it.

So now she could walk, look, see that tan dog lying with its head on its paws in the dust, opening its eyes as she passed, see those faded houses, go on to see an ordinary main street in an ordinary town where people lived and shopped and worked and drove and some even walked, as over there a woman was pushing a stroller with a blonde child, who kept turning around, trying to pull himself out, and his mother said gently then sharply, "Sit there, just sit there."

Here was a Sprouse-Reitz store—she was on the other side of the street from where she walked before—with cutlery and hardware in the window. Here was another small grocery store, its door open wide, with a wooden counter, and canned food on shelves up to the high ceiling. And here was the filling station with several cars waiting for the gas to be pumped by a man in a white hat.

And at this moment the tow truck was coming back, pulling his car—what an inert thing it seemed being dragged so, powerless. She could see him in the cab of the truck with the driver.

Relieved, he looked relieved, as she was now relieved.

CHAPTER

7

"THAT GROCERY STORE WE WENT BY WITH THE HIGH SHELVES," he said, as they sat at the bar in the Gold Rush Hotel, "my father had a store like that when I was a kid. I used to work there after school and on Saturdays. Sometimes I'd have to get a can down from the top shelf—it seemed so high to me—maybe it was eight feet, nine feet— I'd use a long pole with a hook on the end to grasp it, and then drop it down into my other hand— I got so that I could catch it right every time." The palm of his left hand was turned upward, the fingers curved as if to catch a can.

She waited but he did not go on. He ordered another Scotch. He lit a cigarette.

She had known nothing of his story (though he knew everything, or almost everything, of hers), and yet in some way, she thought she knew him. It was a knowing independent of where he was born, what he did as a boy, who his father was, who his mother was— It was a knowing that comes from how someone acts and looks, how he smiles and frowns, when and how he sighs, how he walks and turns, whether he's fast or slow, tense or loose-limbed. . . .

But then here was this statement about his father's store and himself and the grasping hold of the cans on the top shelves, the beginning of facts and sequence. What would she do with this information? Analyze it in terms of the assumption that the child is father to the man? Hoard it for later to be incorporated into a story that was still in the making? But she was not a storyteller. Or rather she was a poor storyteller, tending to doubt the point of her own story once she began to tell it.

"I hope that mechanic knows what he's doing. He's never worked on a Jaguar before," she heard him say. He stubbed his cigarette out. He looked at his watch. "He said to check with him about three. He said he'll know what the problem is by then."

"What if he can't fix it today?" she asked.

"We'll get to that when and if it happens." He ordered another Scotch. The bartender brought his drink and then went back to polishing a gold Cupid at the end of the counter.

"Maybe we'll have to stay over, stay here at the Gold Rush Hotel." He lit another cigarette and smiled at her image in the gilt-framed mirror behind the bar.

To stay over— Then the end of this trip would not be defined as she had defined it, to end after one day and a night and another day. "But it costs fifteen dollars a night to stay here," she blurted out.

He laughed. "How do you know that?"

"The Museum Man told me."

"What Museum Man?"

She told him about the fat man and the museum, making a joke of it, of him. Still, at the end, she added, "I'm being flip about it, but of course, it was not just that. He's got a lot of old tools and things that he claims are from Gold Rush times. You might be interested in it."

"Not at the moment."

She could see he was still thinking about the car, worried about the car.

"He showed me a letter." She told him about the caravan in the desert and what happened to the man who drank too much water.

"It's possible," he said, "that the water was contaminated with some chemical that affected his brain, and he could have been having hallucinations."

"Ah," she said.

She welcomed his comment, his authority. She thought, Yes, that could be what happened. She stared at the glass in her hand. She felt the coldness against her palm. Despite his explanation, she was still clinging to a prior kind of knowing: the racing of her own pulse, as if she were the one running, feeling herself in the running man's body, as he slipped from one circle to the next.

(And all the time, in the mirror, she saw a look on her face, of strain, of exhaustion, as in childbirth.)

He was gazing at her in the mirror. His blue eyes were impenetrable, his face impassive. At this moment, perhaps for the first time, she found his impassivity galling. And yet, at the same time, she needed that very impassivity. It protected her. It limited her. It allowed her to go only so far. To stop running.

At the garage she stood off to the side as he spoke with the mechanic and another man. The hood to the Jaguar was up and the mechanic leaned over and pointed to something in the engine, then stood erect and wiped his hands on a rag, which he put back into his pocket. She watched him as he asked the mechanic a question. She saw the mechanic shake his head.

Once again she was free to stare at him, across the space between them, across the gas pumps, across the cement pooled with dried oil. Once again she was back to longing, the longing she had harbored for so long, the longing she felt before they set out, before this trip was agreed upon. Yet here she was with him, still longing, as if nothing had changed, as if they had not come on this trip. How can you long for what you are in the midst of living through?

"It turns out that it is the fuel pump," he said as he came over to her. "He can't repair it, it has to be replaced with a new one. But he doesn't have the part, and he says it will take him at least a week to get it. Of course, we can't wait. So I've made an arrangement with Vern"—he gestured at the man standing with the mechanic—"to drive us to Sacramento. We can get a plane from there."

It had all been decided without any say on her part, but then, why should she have had any say, it wasn't her car. What mattered, after all, was that this trip—his and hers—would end in the time allotted— a day and a night and another day—no more.

8

SHE WAS IN THE FRONT SEAT OF VERN'S OLD BUICK, IN THE middle, between the two men. He was asking Vern questions, about where he lived, what he did for a living, probing gently, kindly. He was—he could be—very good at that.

Slowly, with a hint of a twang, Vern was telling him about his cabin, five miles out of town. As for work, he said, he did woodcutting. "And on the weekend I pan for gold."

"Do you find any?"

"Very little. But I don't do it for the money. I just like looking for it. I go way back in the hills to places where no one's mined for a long time—a hundred years maybe. I spend the day and then I camp out. Nobody's around. It's nice, it's quiet."

"You go on private land?"

"No. Land owned by the government. Run by the government. The Bureau of Land Management."

He nodded and put his left arm over the back of the seat, behind her. She could feel his shoulder and upper arm through the thin material of his blue and white striped shirt. Hills, meadows, trees slipped by.

Once again he spoke across her. This time he was asking about hunting. His words surprised her. She would not have thought of him as a hunter, would not have liked to have thought of him as someone shooting a defenseless animal. But then what did her thinking have to do with what he was? Yet his thinking had a lot to do with what she was, what she had become.

There was a long silence after the talk of hunting, and she felt his body slacken. Soon his head had fallen to the side and was resting on her shoulder. She had a sense of surrender in him, as if he had finally given up the certainty of control.

She herself had been in a fever of uncertainty, trembling at his touch, trembling when he didn't touch her, a bull in the china shop of her own emotions, ricocheting from fear to pride to fear to judging, her mind saying not this but that, and then not that but this, her bodily responses in sync, out of sync. Now in the presence of a third person, this stranger—a woodcutter, a dabbler in gold mining—all that was over.

She turned to look at Vern. He was a lanky man with red hair. He seemed diffident, faded, like a color print whose color values had muted over the years. Given the outdoor work that he did, one would expect him to be tanned, more robust than he was. She wondered if he had been telling the truth but why should he lie? He did not look like a man who told lies, but then how does a man who lies look?

"Have you been here long?" she asked, abruptly, awkwardly.

"Here?"

"In this area."

"A while," he said. He did not turn his head, but continued to look at the road straight ahead.

"You like it here?"

"Yeah, I do."

A pickup truck was passing them by. In the back of the truck, a large dog, a police dog, was pacing.

"I don't like change all that much," Vern was saying.

He turned to look at her, the expression in his eyes, hungry, eager.

After a moment he added, "Sometimes I've thought about leaving, trying some place else, but—" he turned back to the road, "—I've got all I need here."

He shrugged and with that shrug he seemed to be pulling an extra dense skin over himself, to shut himself in, to shut himself off from others. He acted like someone who had revealed too much, and yet, what had he revealed? Not much.

She turned away from Vern to what mattered to her, to the sense of the weight of his head on her shoulder—it had grown heavier but she did not stir—to the sense of him next to her, a sureness.

Without looking, she could feel his solidity, that alone, no second image, flat, degraded, shadowing him. Her desire to see him in this singular, unclouded way may have been the most intense of all the desires she had for him—and there were many. Strange that this image of him should be so clear, so light-filled in the presence of Vern, a man who seemed to seek obscurity.

Here, now, in this battered car, with their luggage in the backseat piled on top of blankets and boxes and tools and clothes and God knows how much other stuff, he and she were together in a way they had not been before. In the presence of this third. . . .

("There is always a third," the words came to her. She'd read it somewhere, heard it somewhere.)

Gazing at the road ahead, she felt an unaccustomed calmness. Perhaps it had come at this moment because the ending to this trip was now assured: there had been risk, but no consequences, at least of a shattering kind. Yes, she had been wary on this journey, this trial, this whatever. Perhaps there had been, if not a struggle, a jockeying. Now it could be said, she can say, There is no victor, no vanquished.

She looked at the road ahead. Ordinarily, on any return journey, anywhere, she felt an urgent need to count off the miles still to be traveled, as if they were obstacles to be overcome—some weird thing in her brain, in her body, constantly placing the end point at a farther and farther distance. But now she was not counting miles. They were here, they were going on, they would get there.

At the Sacramento airport, they had to wait for several hours for a flight. They sat in the bar, its large windows looking out on the field. Several aircraft, large and small, were parked or fueling. He had a Scotch and then several more. She was not counting in this place that was no more than a way station.

What had been had almost ended.

This was simply a transition.

The cab from the airport stopped in front of his door. The driver was unloading the luggage, he was paying him. She was preparing to say good night. Standing next to him, she could see a sheet of paper had been pinned to his door. In the light from the fixture above the door, the writing was clear enough for her to read.

Dear Edmond:

Where were you? I came at eight as you said. You didn't answer the door or the telephone. I came back at nine and at ten. Call me.

Love, Carol.

He is taking the note down, he is opening the door with his key. She is standing, knowing what she does not want to know, her mind plunging from possibility to certainty: he has made this arrangement, this date—which by mischance he has missed—as insurance, to counteract what he foresaw might happen, an erasure planned ahead of time, to undo whatever would happen on their trip together. Together. She can almost laugh at the word.

I must go to my car, she tells herself, but instead she follows him inside, leaving her bag outside. She is not sure why she is doing what she is doing. She thinks, Maybe I will never know again exactly why I do what I do because of this betrayal—yes, it has to be called that: a betrayal. Judgment is making its brutal claim. She has no intention of stopping it.

She stands dumb before him, wordless. Yet so many words are stuck in her mouth, What? Who? Why? This Carol could be, she flails at herself, a friend, a relative. No, she knows it could not be so. She knows who Carol is, the other, another. . . . What astounds her so is his secrecy. He has had this secret the whole time, knew what awaited him on his return, planned it to be that way. Before this, between them, it was always her secrets at issue.

If he had told her before they left that he had to be back to meet this woman, this Carol, would that have been better? No. Would it have made a difference? Yes.

Yet once again she is propelled by some inner command to take his side, to argue his case. You have no right to condemn him, he has a right to see someone else whenever and wherever he wants to. So she argues with herself, but she is losing the argument. "That note . . . that note on the door. . . ." The words are sounding, strangled with thickness. "I saw the note. . . . You were expecting maybe. . ."

He is saying, "A friend . . . . I should have called her. . . . I forgot. . . ." Is he making this up as she stands before him, looking at him? Now, why, is she thinking at this moment of that other moment when he awoke, surprised? In spite of herself, she has been building a case against him.

I've got to go, she thinks, I've got to put my bag, which is outside— is it safe to leave it there?—in my car and drive home.

"Well," he says, "it's late, after one." He is actually standing before her and saying this, putting out his arm to embrace her, though it is more like a dismissal. The hell with luggage. She is staying.

"I'm not going," the words come out. "I'm staying."

There is an odd glint in his eyes she has never seen before. "You do what you want to do," he shrugs. "I've got to get some sleep."

He goes into the bedroom. She has followed him and is standing watching him. He takes off his clothes. He is turned away from her. She sees the bend in his spine, the flat place above his buttocks. He gets into bed. He covers himself and turns to the wall. She takes off her clothes. She turns off the light. She gets into bed beside him. She is stunned by her own audacity.

It is as if she is erasing, must erase the other, the Carol, this third, by this act. If she does not do it, she will suffer untold anguish. It is as simple as that. By putting herself in this place beside him, it is an assertion that she has been with him, it cannot be denied, that they have been together, yes, together.

In an instant he is snoring lightly. She cannot sleep. She is counting rooms, not sheep, this room, the room in the motel, the room in the

Gold Rush Hotel they could have gone to, fifteen dollars a night, furnished so as to look one hundred years old—

She turns on her back and looks into the darkness. She stares at a corner and thinks of other rooms where angles have narrowed, become more acute angles, where things, doors, objects become taller as well as narrower as they withdraw. . . .

She is going over what she said, what she didn't say. She could have said—why didn't she?—So this is what you were planning, a betrayal. . . . She should have said, We have to talk about this. He would have said, I can't. It's too late. I'm tired.

It would have had the same ending.

She turns on her left side. She puts her right arm around him. There is the same smell of his skin as in the motel cabin, the alcohol coming off it, being excreted through his skin. She tightens her arm around him—like a boa constrictor, or like someone holding on for dear life. Dear life? I am losing it, losing him, she thinks, but I am holding on nevertheless, as tightly as I can.

She could almost laugh. A savage laugh. There has come to her, for no reason a scene in a Marx Brothers movie, *A Day at the Races*, yes, *A Day at the Races*—Groucho is holding a blonde woman in his arms. She says, Hold me closer, closer, and Groucho says, If I hold you any closer, I'll be in back of you—or was it on the other side of you?

The other side of him.

How many are there?

I must get up, she tells herself. This is bad for me. No, it's not bad. It's simply what I'm doing. I'm following out my life and life is—life is— She can't say what life is, though some old reflex in her mind holds mockingly to a memorized fragment from her school days: "Life is real, life is earnest, and the grave is not its goal. . . ."

And then the thought—where are these things coming from?—a

thought horrified by its own thinking—the thought, the image of a cradle, of the "rocking the cradle" that she saw in that "museum," only this time it is not a cradle rocking but a bier with a tiny body laid out on it, wrapped in a cloth, a tiny face painted on the cloth, and dirt is being dug up, is being flung upon it, covering it—

It could be—is—Julie's face, her child's face, on that bier— All this time, since they set out, she has not thought of her once. It is only that I have been thinking of other things, she tries to excuse herself, but it does not wash, does not alter her own judgment upon herself.

Now in collusion with punishment, in agreement to sentencing, she pulls her arm away. She sits up. Julie is safe, she reminds herself, she is with Joan, staying over with Joan, next door. Still there is revulsion at her own mind, at its playing with the image of death when there has been no death. Was it a kind of trickery, a wish to feel death? Was it because desire has gotten hold of her, has preempted everything else, and in its greed, refuses any and all limits?

At the thought of desire, now, even now, desire is building in her, growing, while he, sleeping, faces away from her. She could touch him to bring him to response. No, she will not touch him, that is against something in her, that without consent, while he is asleep, she is taking advantage— But who has the advantage in this, she does not know. Besides, sex is not what she wants from him at this moment.

I must go, she thinks. But to get up, to leave, is no simple action. It is like tearing herself away from being bound, from having chosen to be bound.

She gets up. In the darkness she takes her bra from the chair where she has thrown it. She puts it on. She takes her panties. She puts them on. Each action leads to the next action, each thing to the next thing, to shirt, to shorts, to sandals.

She turns on the light. He does not stir. He is lying there, turned to the wall, he himself a wall, a barrier. She turns off the light.

She goes into the living room. The light is still on. The note that was on the door is lying on the table, where he dropped it. She picks it up. She reads it again. She will write, in imitation of Carol who can say his name, write his name so easily. She will say—

"Dear—" (She hurls herself against his name.)

"Dear Edmond:

"I—what?

"You—what?

"Love, Lorle."

Love?

She will not write.

She closes the door behind her. She picks up her bag. Nobody took it after all. Why would anybody take it at this time of night? She goes to her car, parked in his parking space. She starts the engine, backs out, and drives down the alley. At Middlefield Road she turns left to go south.

There is no one else on the road, which is newly paved and brightly lit. Everything seems silent, muted. She comes to a red light. She stops. No one is coming from the cross street. Still she waits in obedience to the law, a simple law, not to be broken.

In the stillness this intersection, which she has gone through how many hundreds of times, is no longer familiar. Off to each side of the road, tract houses are solidly shuttered. In them all are sleeping, as back there he is sleeping. And if he is dreaming, what dreams does he dream? Wish-fulfilled dreams of a woman—what woman—?

She is waiting for the light to change as if it would be an answer, and if not an answer a hope, though she cannot believe that hope is an answer.

The light changes to green. Her foot is on the accelerator, pressing down. The car speeds forward. She passes Mitchell Park, she passes the Children's Center, she passes the Library. She turns right on Charleston Road, then left on Nelson Drive. Just before she turns into her own street, she thinks of the trip he will be making, alone. He will take the plane to Sacramento, he will get off the plane and be met by Vern, who will drive him on valley roads . . . they will pass a burning mound. . . .

9

WHEN EDMOND GOT OFF THE PSA FLIGHT IN SACRAMENTO, he looked for Vern at the gate. He didn't see him among the people standing or those milling about. Damn, he told me he'd be here, now I'll have to rent a car, and drop it off there, if they let me drop it off there, God knows what the drop-off fee will be.

But suddenly there was Vern in front of him, waving, as if to say, I am here, I've been here. He'd remembered him as having lighter hair. He also remembered him as being shorter.

"Been waiting long?" he asked, and shook hands a little too heartily.

"An hour, maybe a little more. I don't mind. I like airports." He offered to take the box with the fuel pump that Edmond was carrying.

"It's all right. It's not heavy."

"Do you have any other baggage?"

"No, I'm planning on driving back today. Mac said once I brought the part, he could fix the car right away, in an hour or so."

"Maybe a little more than an hour, if I know Mac."

They walked to the parking lot. "My car's just over there," Vern pointed.

The car was easy to recognize, a beat-up blue Buick, with all the things still piled in the backseat, as if Vern were planning to take off at any moment.

His eyes on the road ahead, Vern made no attempt at small talk. Grateful for the silence, Edmond leaned back in the seat. The air, coming through the open windows, was already warm. The neat rectangles of farmland were giving way to rolling hills. He felt relieved that everything had gone so smoothly. The dealer had the fuel pump in stock, he'd picked it up first thing this morning, the plane left on time and arrived on time, Vern was waiting, as he said he'd be. Now, all that remained was to get the car fixed and drive it home.

Lulled by the warmth and by the sound of the wheels on the road, he closed his eyes and began to doze. In an instant he came awake, saying, "What—?"

"I didn't say anything," Vern said.

"I thought you did," Edmond mumbled, even as he clutched at the fading image of some woman, what woman, a woman with her belly torn open and a terrible smell coming from it. He sat up, he forced himself to attention, to stick with this, where he was, moving forward on this road, with Vern, in this car, he'd stay on the surface, keep to the surface, the hell with probing depths, his own or others.

He asked Vern how long he'd had the Buick. He said that he'd bought it used two years ago. He asked if he'd had any trouble with it.

"No, no trouble. The engine is in very good condition. The tires are good. The brakes are okay. Only the upholstery needs to be redone. You can see where the leather is torn in places. I'll get around to it sometime soon, maybe this winter."

"How is it here in the winter? Much snow?"

"Not much. We're low for real snow."

After a long silence—more meadows, more hills, a sudden rocky escarpment in the distance—Vern, still looking straight ahead, asked, "What do you do?"

"Do?"

"What kind of work do you do?"

"I'm a doctor."

He didn't volunteer anything.

At the garage he handed over the fuel pump to Mac. "What time should I pick up the car?"

"You better give me till five."

"You said it'd only take an hour or so."

"I've got three people here before you that I didn't expect. And I want to make sure I check it out, so you won't have no more trouble on the road."

"You're sure it'll be done by then?"

"It'll be done."

"Damn it," he said to Vern, who had been standing off to the side, "now I've got to waste five hours, when he should have been able to put in the goddammed thing in an hour."

"You'll notice that people around here are not in that much of a hurry."

"So I see." But then he said to himself, What's the hurry, after all? I'll get back tonight in any case. "How about a drink and some lunch?" he asked Vern.

"Why don't you come on out to my place? We can drink a few beers, and I'll barbecue you a hamburger."

When Edmond hesitated, he said, "Come on. Might as well. Better than anything you'll get in town, I guarantee you."

Given the appearance of Vern's car, he never would have thought Vern would have a place like this, so neat and well tended, the small kitchen so orderly, with pots and pans hanging on hooks. He even had a vegetable garden in the back, planted in careful rows.

While Vern set up the barbecue, he sat at a table under the over-hang behind the cabin and had a beer. Looking out on the garden, surrounded by trees, he listened to the sound of insects buzzing, a sound far-off and near, high and low. He heard a chirping sound, cicadas or crickets, he wasn't sure. If they were cicadas, only the male made that sound, he remembered.

Unexpectedly he felt at ease, slowed down in this benign place. And when Vern served the food, there was something comforting in that too, oddly decorous in the way he did it, as if each detail mattered, as if there was a kind of feminine care that was involved here, but masculine as well. A kind of tenderness at the core of it, a caring for things, fixing things, making things right in the world, a world in which things could be made right.

"The hamburgers are great," he said.

Vern nodded, obviously pleased.

"This is really a terrific place you've got here, Vern."

"Yeah, I like it."

"Sometimes I think I ought to try living like this, you know, living the simple life."

"Simple?" Vern said.

"Well, you know what I mean, get rid of what doesn't matter—get down to what does. . . ."

Vern nodded.

"Living by yourself, you don't get lonely out here?"

"No. Though I'm thinking of getting a dog for company."

Abruptly he got up and went inside the cabin, then came out with a photo. A much younger Vern, in shorts, was holding a white dog with a black spot on its face. "That's me, with Spot, during the war. In the Pacific. He was some smart dog, a mutt, any trick you tried to teach him, he'd learn it in a minute. They wouldn't let me take him when I left."

"So you're looking for another Spot." Edmond smiled.

"Not really. Spot was the right dog for then, but I don't think he'd be right for here. No, I'm thinking of looking for a hunting dog, so I can take him hunting with me. . . ."

"You'd take him gold panning too?"

"I don't know. I'll see. I take things as they come." He was silent for a moment, looking around the garden. "I've got a good setup here. I've got no cause for complaint."

"Seems like a great setup to me."

"Were you in the war?" Vern asked, as he started to clean up.

"I was." He started to get up.

"No, no, you sit there, I'll take care of it. What branch?"

"The Army."

"An officer?"

He nodded.

While Vern was inside, he sat quietly, becalmed in the pleasure of looking at trees, and at low green things in the sun. He felt a sudden stirring in himself, a surrendering to something sensual but not sexual. A letting go into the unfamiliar . . . the strangeness of comfort.

Vern appeared, holding a dish towel.

"Nice out here," Edmond said.

Vern nodded.

"Peaceful."

Yes, peaceful. He felt as if a great weight had been lifted off him. It was like a sudden absolution from the constant pressure of regret. He wasn't thinking of the past or even of the future but only of now.

Vern folded the towel. "What kind of a doctor are you?"

"What kind do you think?"

Vern shrugged. "I have no idea."

"I'm a psychiatrist—a psychoanalyst."

"Oh," Vern said, and paused. Edmond saw in Vern's eyes—he had seen it how many times before in others when he said what he did—the sudden shift in focus, from near to middle distance and back again. First something like awe, then a moving away, and then a coming back.

"Were you a psychiatrist during the war?"

"No, I did my training afterward."

"I almost saw a psychiatrist once."

"But you didn't?"

"No, I didn't."

So now would come the inevitable telling. Each one had his story, some incident, some trauma. He had not expected it from Vern, yet here he was, already having embarked on telling what had happened to him in the Pacific.

"It wasn't such a big deal, but they did send me back for R and R afterward. I was doing a routine mechanical check on one of the planes. My buddy Ned came by and wanted me to do something with him, I can't remember what, but I said I still had some checking to do and he said he'd help me, what should he do, and I pointed up to the cockpit and told him. So Ned climbed up, and I kept working under the wing, and I heard this plane come in real low, it was one of our planes but I couldn't see it because of where I was. Then I finished, and I didn't see Ned up there, I figured he must have left, so I left, and after a while I said, Anybody see Ned? And then I found out that the plane that came in had been on fire. It was so low, and Ned was right there. It killed him, just like that. Later I thought, He was killed instead of me, it should have been me. It kept bothering me that I walked away that way, that I figured he had left, when he wasn't the kind of guy who would leave without telling me."

After a silence, Edmond said, "You must have been a kid then."

"I was eighteen. I'd gone into the service early, lied about my age—they were going to send me to talk to someone—but I got over it—they reassigned me, to another place—a different island—the one with Spot—that came afterward—I got over it—you get over things. I guess you hear lots of stories, all the time."

He didn't say yes, he didn't say no. "Every story's different."

And the same, he said to himself, as Vern went back into the house.

In that interval of listening the pounding had started, he could feel and hear it in his head, his chest, staging its protest at having to listen to more suffering and more guilt—more guilt and more suffering.

More clearly than ever, he could see why some do mad things, throw things over, throw their whole lives over to get out from under.

Vern reappeared, carrying the dish towel, which he hung over a railing to dry in the sun.

"What's that shed?" Edmond pointed, gulling himself back to where he had been before the telling.

"That's where I keep my prospecting gear. Like to see it?"

He followed Vern as he went over to the shed at the rear of the garden and opened the door. Here, too, everything was in order. Sorted out on shelves were an axe, a saw, a pick, a long-handled, round, pointed shovel, manila rope, an acetylene lamp, a can of car-bide, flashlights, a canteen, jars with nails, some cold chisels, a mortar and a pestle. . . . Vern's mining clothes were hung up neatly on hooks. His boots were on the floor.

"Looks as though you're ready to go."

"Anytime I feel like it, I just get my gear and I'm off."

"Must be great."

"It is. You should come some time with me. You'd like it."

"Maybe I will."

"You could come up and we'd go prospecting and hunting—make a week of it."

Edmond looked around. "You don't keep your guns here."

"No, no. They're locked up. I wouldn't leave them lying about." As he closed the shed door, he said, "I mean it. You ought to think about coming up here for a few days. You look like you could use a change."

"Do I?"

"Well, you know, I mean, who am I to tell the doctor?"

It was amazing how the fact that the car was fixed made the world seem pliable. At each curve in the road, he felt the lean in his own body, he and the car moving as one. . . .

Just before he reached the Bay Bridge, he ran into heavy traffic, and the Jaguar was forced to a crawl. At least he had come to a decision. It was so clear in his mind, he felt as if he'd already acted upon it. He was going to tell her that it had to be over between them.

During most of the trip he'd managed to put her out of his mind, until, when Vern was driving him to the garage, he said, "That girl . . ."

"What girl?"

"The girl that was with you."

"Oh. Yes."

"She's not your wife."

"No, not my wife."

"What's her name again?"

He told him her name.

"Good-looking, she's very good-looking."

"Yes."

"She has odd eyes."

"What do you mean?"

"The way they stare. Like a cat. She moves a little like a cat too. You known her long?"

"Long, short, it's hard to say."

"I had the feeling—I hope you don't mind my saying—that maybe you two had a fight."

"Why do you say that?"

"I don't know . . . I just thought . . ."

"No, no fight," he'd said.

No, he thought as he neared the tollbooth, we did not have a fight. It was different from fighting. It was more like fending off grasping. She was grasping and I was fending off. Wasn't that what it was? But I'm not going to spend time thinking of what it was or wasn't. I've made my decision.

Driving south on Highway 101—the traffic was moving more rapidly now—he passed empty fields, he passed the naked structures of industrial buildings just going up.

He thought of risk, of all that he had risked, for no reason, for God knows how many reasons. When it's all over, he'll be able to distance himself, look at what he did with some objectivity, analyze why—

The car breaking down like that was a warning to stop before it went too far. Or had it already gone too far? He should never have done what he did. It was his fault, far more than hers. But he can't help thinking of the way she acted that night when they came back and she saw the note on the door. After all that time in analysis, he thought she was better, but still—she was a hysteric.

He is remembering what Sullivan wrote about hysterics, Sullivan who, of all of them, wrote with the most clarity, so directly, not caught up in the jargon. His clinical insights were brilliant. He'd said that hysterics led a kind of pseudo-life, always dramatizing, exaggerating, using other people as shadowy figures, as an audience for their own performance, they shifted so quickly, one moment they were in the depths of despair and the next in a kind of euphoria, as if they were constantly acting out a fiction that had little if any relevance to real life—

And somehow he had gotten caught up in that fiction.

↷ 10 ↶

ANOTHER DAY HAD GONE BY, THE THIRD DAY, AND HE HAD not called. She told herself, I will wait and get through this day. This is called managing. I manage to get through the day. Acting like normal. What was normal? Normal was to protect her child, to protect her as much as she could even, especially, from this hidden life of hers that kept threatening to possess her.

If there was a kind of deception, all right, a kind of lie, laced into this care, so be it. When she was with Julie she must hold back the other life, not let it come through. To do so was, in a way, a cutting off of herself from her child, but she had to choose between protecting her and cutting her off, and not cutting her off and letting her be exposed to what she herself could barely contend with.

Still, of course, she was always on the alert, waiting for the phone to ring. And when it rang, the moment before answering was like a dread vastness, across which she leaped into a kind of faith that it would be he calling. But when she heard the voice of another who was not he, then she felt despair, which she struggled not to show, managing, still managing, to say proper words, apt words. . . .

Wait, wait, she cautioned herself, if you need to, you can call him tomorrow, but hold off the calling for now. For he needs time, or so it seems. Just as you hate the passage of this time, he needs it. Yes, she must try to think as he thinks.

She seized on the thought of the trip to Mexico, how without even a moment of thought, when he suggested it, she immediately said no, she would not go. Yet why had he wanted to go there? She'd never asked herself that question. It felt at the time like a simple judgment on her part. A place too far, too strange, she judged it, and dismissed it out of hand. But now, she wondered, what kind of judgment was it? Something in her had made that assessment, a calculation in advance. Too much strangeness.

Could he not have thought, and with some justification, that she would not go with him to Mexico because she did not trust him enough? So then was it true that her trust in him was not absolute, but only conditional, that she had in this sense failed him, betrayed him?

And here came another leap of thought: to the recognition that hers may have been the first betrayal, and his the second, but there were many more yet to come, so that this—whatever this was that she was in with him—would be nothing but a series of betrayals of each other, hidden in words, erupting in actions, buried in failure to act.

On the fifth day at five in the afternoon he called. At the sound of his voice all waiting was erased, as if it was no more than an experience owed, a payment in advance on what was to come.

"Are you free tonight?"

Yes, she said.

Could he come over?

Yes, she said.

About nine?

Yes, about nine.

She hung up and stood for a moment, staring at the black telephone mounted on the wall. After the thought of betrayal, in compensation for betrayal, in blessed relief from betrayal, after all the waiting (and anxiety), now there would be only a short wait, four hours (and certainty). She did not have to know, maybe she did not even want to know, exactly what would happen.

She flooded his image, the image of the one who would be here in four hours, with a heightened brilliance of color, thrilling to that image, falling into the voluptuous depth and width of how it would be when he came to her door.

When she opened the door and saw him standing there, she stood for a moment and stared at him, almost savagely, as if to ask, What can eyes ferret out? This was real, it was no fantasy, she was actually seeing him, a man she knew and didn't know—that thought, too, increasing desire.

He came inside her house. He had not been here before but he barely looked around, as if he did not want to become familiar with her surroundings. She asked him about the car. He told her about the car. They were having a car conversation, about what was wrong, about how it was fixed. She could not believe that they were having a car conversation, when so much else was at stake. Yet she was taking part in this conversation, responding yes, no, and really, when needed.

He told her that Vern had picked him up at the airport. He told her that he had to wait for five hours but then finally the car was ready, and he drove back. No, he had no trouble on the way back. It was a pleasure, a pleasure to drive—no trouble—he loved to drive.

"I remember you said that and you also said you never had an accident."

"You remember my words so exactly?"

"You don't say that many words."

He laughed and looked around as if he was searching for something, an exit maybe. And suddenly she felt pity for him. But desire has no room for pity, she knew. She wanted to throw herself at him. She didn't. She told herself, It is probably better to wait, though God knows what is better and not better between us.

He was speaking again of his trip, of the time he spent with Vern. She was listening but something was being omitted that needed inclusion in this foreplay, yet he was acting as if it were complete. It was missing something left over from the last time they were together, that unfinished business, once again unfinished for all her reasoning with herself that she must think as he thinks, be on his side. The name Carol on a piece of paper, Love, Carol. She should ask him about her. But she cannot. It is, she now sees, as if there is no such thing as things going on here. Each time they must start anew, as if they share no past at all, not the just past, nor the past that extended for months, even years.

This is a new way of being, she said to herself. Accept that you have no claim on him. You know he has a wife—you know they are separated—a temporary separation, he said that when we began. But this other woman, this Carol, who and what is she? Perhaps she is an antidote to me, calm, adaptable, accepting. Perhaps she is protection from me.

And if I am a threat to him, then why is he here?

Out of desire.

Perhaps, though desire uses everything else for its purposes.

"The child is asleep?"

"Yes. Julie." She needed to pronounce the name. It was like a safeguard.

"I wouldn't want—"

"Yes, I am sure she's asleep."

As it was a cool night, she had lit a fire. They sat on the couch. She had poured the wine into glasses, placed them on the coffee table in front of them.

"So you think I have been silent," he said.

"Not always. You talked—about—about history—about the Gold Rush—" She laughed, a little.

"That didn't interest you?"

"No, no, I wouldn't say that. It's just that—" She stopped and waited.

"What kind of conversation did you want from me?"

"I thought, perhaps, about—about what was happening—"

"Does it have to be spoken of?"

The dry wood was crackling in the fireplace; sparks were soaring up the chimney. She was aware of a buzzing in her head. From one glass of wine, how could that be? Everything she looked at was through a more intense overlay of color, in this place, her own living room. That gray wall, that red chair, that ocher rug. The colors sharp and defined.

"There is something I have to say to you."

She waited.

"It's so warm in here."

"I can open the door."

She opened the sliding glass door to the patio. Outside in the garden, the trees were massed in darkness. There was no moon. The fog had drifted in from over the hills, from the ocean beyond. Trembling, she returned to the couch and sat beside him. He was staring at the fire. He did not turn to her.

"I noticed, I couldn't help noticing," he said, "the stain on your shirt, under your arms, where you are sweating."

She was stunned. No, she had never expected these words—other words, perhaps, but not these.

Yes, she was sweating, the sweat staining this crimson silk shirt. It was only part of the liquefaction that was going on in her, between her legs, within her crotch, inside her, she was swelling with moisture . . . hot and wet, when she looked at him, was beside him. . . .

Why these words to her? It was like an attack, on her body, the flaws in her body, in her being.

But when he said it, there was an agony in his voice, as if it was being drawn from him, out of some deep recess, as if it was against himself, somehow.

She told herself, I must see what he is doing. Now I am the one listening. That is what he did for me, he listened. But he is no longer listening to me.

A small rage shuddered through her. Once, the first time he saw her naked, he said to her, You are so perfectly formed. Is it that he is seeing in her a failure of perfection?

And what is she seeing in him?

She said, "It is warm in here."

She did not say, Yes, I sweat, of course I sweat, like anyone else. But the thought of saying it made her feel she would not let him provoke her, out of some strange revulsion, some strange anxiety, some strange—

And then, with a sudden groan, he turned and took her—against himself, he was going against himself? she did not care. (What is care here?) She needed him, she wanted him, whatever would come. . . .

She could still endow him with tenderness to make herself the object of his tenderness.

She thrust aside all that could be explained in psychoanalytic terms. Against this system of thought she had already taken the trip, taken the risk, refused the laws, The Law, as propounded to her, calling on something soaring, a moment's excuse, a moment's softness, and somewhere a hidden sob.

So many ways of being, of feeling, this replacing that, that replacing this, in a random circling of thought.

If it felt like deliverance, it felt like a form of sacrifice, a propitiation of some god or other, a sacred object to be brought down—through love.

༕ II ༖

AT HOME HE COULD NOT SLEEP. HE HAD A DRINK AND another drink, waiting for release, or at least numbness. But he could not stop going over what he said, what he did not say.

When he walked up to her door, he intended to say to her that they had to stop. He rang the doorbell. She opened the door. He looked at her. And then—

He found himself saying, "Vern met me. . . . I had to wait five hours. . . . He did a good job. . . . The car . . . The car . . ." He was holding himself steady that way. After a while he would say what he had to say. But when he was sitting on the couch beside her, even as he looked into the fire, other thoughts kept spurting up like flames, shriveling words.

He thought, This is her house.

He thought, I have invaded it, am being invaded by it.

He thought of the child, Julie, sleeping. He felt a sudden jealousy.

He did not have to turn to see the unappeased longing in her. He knew he could never appease it. He knew he must separate himself from her. He would simply say, I can't take it anymore. But if he said that, then he would have to explain, but he didn't want to—couldn't explain.

Wouldn't it be better to lie to her? Better for her. She'd be able to salvage something if she could be convinced that it wasn't his choice, that he wasn't rejecting her, rather it was the circumstances of his life that demanded this break. Yes, it would be better to lie, to say that Jean—his wife—was coming back sooner than he thought, they were going to try again. He had to break it off now.

But he was bound by an unforgiving necessity not to lie to her.

And then when he saw the sweat under her arms, wetting the dark red blouse, he did not lie. He had to tell her what he saw, the animal stain. He waited after he told her that, and told himself in the resulting silence, Now she is going to be angry. Now she will throw me out. Now that will end it, she will end it. So it will not be I who ended it. But she simply said, It is warm in here.

Then this jumped to that. There was desire. There was need—

He could feel her desire for him, he was falling into the wetness of her desire, she so moist, welcoming—yes, she sweats—that revulsion whose other face is intense desire—yes, yes, he knew all about that—but knowing did not abate either desire or revulsion. Instead, revulsion inflamed desire, desire fed on revulsion. . . .

He thrust himself upon her greedily, and at the same time it was as if he was taking shelter in her. He kept trying to hold to the thought that they must not be melded, he must refuse it—so much refusal was needed. To give in would be a small death, a dissolution, one wouldn't want to be dissolved. . . .

And then—yet another and then—in the next instant, seized by the most intense pleasure he shuddered as he came and cried out, "I told you I'd fuck you, you bitch!"

He stared at the stain on the carpet, dark gray against lighter gray, an island with an irregular coastline in the midst of a sea. It was stained when he moved in—after he left the house—his house and Jean's house—

"I told you I'd fuck you . . ."

Who was the "you"? Jean? Carol? Her?—Lorle?—still that difficulty with her name. (Was it a made up name? He never asked her.) Did she hear it? She gave no sign of hearing it.

Unintended words? No. He believed intention could be found, could always be found, if one dredged deeply enough, patiently enough to undo the resistance. But that cry that came as he came was the very testing and taunting of that belief.

With her, in sex with her, he had it both ways, all ways, condemned himself and escaped, found innocence and renounced it, believed and refused belief.

He got up and had another drink. In the clarity that liquor soon brought—that point of clarity reached before the rapid slide into soddenness—he was able to think: What had all this been but acting out? He didn't need anybody to tell him that, he knew that, and yet he went on with her even as he told himself he would not. Was she no more than an object to him, the present object of his libido?

The present object of his libido—prepared words, waiting to be applied on the proper occasion.

This was not the proper occasion.

"I told you I'd fuck you . . ."

He was still being flayed, flaying himself with words that, once said, had been engraved on his brain, to be pored over again and again. Now these same words were migrating to his skin for all to read: the outward signs of an inner life. As saints bleed, so he was bleeding but there was no saintliness here, only the rawness of words. Like thorns.

He wondered if he could be going mad, losing the fundamental notion of his being, of anyone's being.

No, he knew he was not mad.

There was only—only?—the threat of anxiety, waiting in the shadows, ready to spring, ready to thrust him into a world of shallow light, of disconnection.

Three months ago it had seized him without warning, had shaken him, but then had eased off, as swiftly as it had come. Having attacked once, it could attack again in its own time, that he knew, no matter how much he would try to fend it off.

He had another drink and then another drink. He was already beginning to fall into relief, more than relief, into the ease of accepted shame. He was driving himself past a lot, maybe past everything. There was exhilaration in leaving it all behind.

CHAPTER

⌐ 12 ⌐

YES, SHE HAD HEARD THOSE WORDS, BUT NO, SHE HAD NOT yet left them behind. They surfaced when least expected, sometimes when she was still, sometimes when she was moving. They hung in the air as if they were waiting, but not for an answer. She told herself that she was learning something new, to know something and not know it at the same time.

Admittedly, certain questions were being omitted, in particular, the ones that began, What if he . . . ? As a consequence, she felt oddly unassailable, able to take what seemed like a larger view. Men say odd things at the moment of climax, she told herself. Some grunt, some shout, some groan, some even sneeze. A physiological response. She could see that, accept that. It was surely better to accept that, better in the sense of not threatening to destroy what she was in. For it felt like an enclosure, this—this affair—this whatever it was, and she was inside it, contained by it, held up by it.

At this moment Julie came into the bedroom trailing her blanket and got into bed with her. She curved her body around her child's small body, holding her as if she were the one being encircled.

Some things, some actions, once decided upon, once initiated, can be relied on to proceed on their own to a necessary ending. As now she was folding the clothes, having taken them from the dryer, socks, T-shirts, pants were being folded, the action initiated by habit, they were being put away in drawers, where they belonged. As now she was washing the dishes, having set the dirty dishes on the counter to her right, then washing them in the dishpan filled with soap, then rinsing them in the water from the faucet, then placing them on the rack to her left.

Other things seem to come with scant prodding, stay, go, come back again, with no end in sight. As now she was hearing the words—the two sets of words—one about her sweating, ". . . the stain . . . under your arms . . . ," torn out of him as if it were agony to say the words—and the other set of words—"I told you I'd fuck you, you bitch," and she had to ask, Was that, too, agony? It hadn't sounded like agony.

Sweating, yes, she sweated, what was it he wanted, for God's sake, perfection, no sweating, an ice-cold being, a Snow Queen, which she was far from being? And was he exacting revenge for that? Or for what?

And the second set of words? In the grip of passion she had been able to ward them off, able to overcome doubt and the corrosive judgment of mind. Though she had heard him say the words, she had not credited them to him, as she had not really credited the howling to him. It was necessary to hold back the too crudely defined, to allow ambiguity—what was and what wasn't at the same time—to accept that meaning can be this or that—to accept that words are malleable—

But what if? What if the words were proof of some hidden aggression in him, now being let loose, loosed upon her, against her? For what? For refusing him? But she hadn't refused him. Or, if not against her, for her to witness, for her to be witness to, if not judge of.

In the night she kept falling into sleep and waking up, and falling into sleep and waking up, caught in a repeating dream—she was trying to fix something but she could not get it right, always the same dream with the same ending taking her into the same beginning, trying to fix something—

They have driven over the hills to the coast and then south to San Gregorio Beach. It is not a warm day, the fog is in, so they have settled into a small hollow in a dune out of the wind. From there they can see the water, rolling, gray, not pacific.

While the two girls, Julie and Melanie, have been climbing to the top of the next dune and then throwing themselves down, shouting with glee, she and Patricia have been speaking of a proposal before the town council, a plan for fair housing, and about what can they do to help with its passage.

"We're hungry," the girls are clamoring.

"You want lunch already? It's not even noon."

"We're really hungry," they say.

She and Patricia portion out celery and carrot sticks, and small pieces of roast chicken. Julie drops her chicken leg in the sand, and almost at once a single gull appears, circling above them, not yet certain but getting bolder. Julie, half frightened, wanting to touch him, unable to touch him, shrieks each time the bird alights nearby. And finally, in a bold swoop, it darts down and snaps up the chicken leg, struggling with it in its beak, as it rises rapidly in the air.

"He took my chicken," Julie says mournfully but also pleased.

"It's okay," says Patricia. "Here's another one."

"I want another one too," says Melanie.

"Finish the one you have first, then I'll give you another one."

"Don't drop it this time," Lorle says.

And then, of course, Julie drops it.

"I didn't mean to. It just fell." She picks it up and starts to scrape the sand away with her fingers.

"I have some water with me," Patricia offers, "I'll rinse the sand off."

After she rinses it, she gives it back to Julie, who bites into it and makes a face. "It's getting sand in my teeth. I don't want it," she says, looking around for the gull that has been crying overhead.

Lorle has heard Patricia laugh and say, "Give it to me."

Or rather it is as if she has overheard it, even as she is listening to other words: "The stain . . . under your arms . . . ," "I told you I'd . . ."

Under an immense gray sky mirroring an immense gray sea, the wind has begun to blow harder. Even here in the shelter of the dune, she can feel it thrusting up sand, sharp against her cheekbones. Waves are breaking on the shore, breaking up the sound of his words as they come and go. She thinks she sees something way out in the water, a small dark thing bobbing up and down, not moving forward, always in the same place. She looks again, and it is gone.

"Are you ready for brownies?" she asks the girls.

"Yes, yes," they both say.

"You look cold," she says to Julie, who is shivering.

"I'm not cold."

"How about putting on your jacket anyhow? Come on, I'll help you."

To put a jacket on a child, your child, is such a simple clear act, even though Julie wiggles. When she has finished zipping it up, she puts her arms around her and hugs her.

They are walking along the water's edge. The girls are running ahead. Barefoot, they follow the action of the waves, in, then out, in, then out.

Patricia has dropped her voice, her tone is that of one revealing a secret, yet playfully. She is telling of going to the city, of meeting a man there. It is all very pleasurable, lighthearted, not serious. Mark, her husband, doesn't care that much for sex, she says, so she feels free to look for it elsewhere.

Why is she telling me this? Lorle wonders. A confidence offered in expectation of a confidence in return. But what is there for her to say? He said, "I told you I'd fuck you, you bitch." Or I had a dream last night that I couldn't get out of.

At the edge of the water a flock of small shorebirds are running in and out with the tide, pecking quickly and lightly at what lies beneath the wet sand—worms, tiny crabs hiding—and then, in the next instant, as if startled, they rise up into the air in a tight formation, following some leader or other, and the water coming in has covered their tiny tracks, and once again the water is receding, and they are alighting.

Something is happening to her here on San Gregorio Beach in the aftermath of a secret told—and a secret not told. In this world of sea and sky she is weighing things in the balance, and has found her own judgment wanting. He is just a human being, for God's sake. In her mind she has made him too large. What a burden that must be for him. For all her so-called watching, she has not been able to see him as he is. It is the greed in her own desire, that "I want—I want—I want—" that has blinded her.

She has a sudden rush of tenderness. Not awe, but tenderness. She has as well a sense of danger for him and for herself, if they cannot get through this crucial moment.

At home, after she put Julie to bed, she felt she had to write to him, this minute, to explain to him this revelation, for it seemed like a revelation this whatever she had found at San Gregorio, the possibility of a largeness of spirit, as if the sea and the sky in their largeness, in their generosity, had entered into her. It was almost exaltation, a conviction that even as you lost, whatever you lost, you could still set things straight through decency.

She had not written to him before. Words came, words that were not what she wanted to say. She hesitated. She began again. They seemed raw, awkward, they did not convey what she was feeling, there was no corroboration in them of the vastness that had come into her, or of the danger she felt. Still she persisted.

Dear Edmond:

What I have to say to you I am saying in a letter because when we are together it is impossible for me to say what I want to say. It is perhaps sex that stops me from saying. I don't know. I do know that when we began this [she is about to write "affair" —but she cannot use that word]—we began under certain conditions. I know we agreed it would just be for a short while. You said it and I accepted it. But now, in the time remaining to us, it is necessary to be straight with one another. Otherwise what will have come out of this? Some terrible guilt, so that later, looking back, we will feel shame. I think we must be able to face things. Then afterward we will be able to say we did what we did, at least in that time we were fair to one another.

And then she added, for she was still not satisfied with what she had written:

I have a feeling that you are constantly testing me, testing to see how far you can go with me to perhaps drive me away. I want to say to you, There is nothing that you can say or do that will stop me from loving you.

Even as she wrote these words, she said to herself, Yes, it is true, I do love him. It was the writing that confirmed this for her, it was the words that proved it was so.

CHAPTER

~ 13 ~

HE READ HER LETTER QUICKLY AND SAID TO HIMSELF, SHE IS better, there is no doubt about that. The hysterical patient who came to him, belittling herself, unsure of her own worth—she is not that anymore. She is straightforward, she even expects that from others, from him. Well, then, she will get that from him.

Later, his last patient gone for the day, he picked up the letter again. Rereading, he felt a small spasm. There was a doubleness in the tone, beneath the call for decency something else, some quality of hubris or sanctimoniousness that resonated with a suggestion of taking over that he did not like. That she should tell him, " . . . it is necessary to . . . we must be able. . . ."

He looked at the words again, critically. They were a weight to him and a sting. He sensed the falseness in them and the duplicity. She was still acting, how could she not, only what part was she taking this time with her protestations of love? This wasn't love and couldn't be. In the final analysis, it was nothing but transference, he knew that, but in a sudden reversal, which made it even worse, she was now taking on the role of comforter and challenger, saying, "We must be able to face . . . ," meaning "You must face . . . ," as if she were the analyst— her version of the analyst—an assumed magnanimity, that was really malign with its hint of mocking words.

How did I never see this before? he wondered. I saw the intensity, I never saw the aggressiveness, the destructiveness. He had to admit his own complicity in this, his own failure. What a damn fool he had been.

Fast upon this anger with himself came another onslaught, disgust with the world. He knew he was going too far but everything else had gone too far, why not this? It had gone too far with Jean. She had called early this morning. She had decided to stay in Paris two months longer. He was paying the bills but she had decided without consulting him. He objected, but not strenuously. It was one more excuse for putting off their so-called reconciliation.

In this, as in everything, he was stuck, unmoving, prey to others' desires and needs, no way out that he could see. He tried to examine what he had done, examine his own motives, but it was like search- ing in the dark, his hand held out, warding off obstacles, the exami- nation itself the obstacle. How was this possible, after all he had been through, the years of work on himself and with others, how was it possible that he had come to this?

Her voice, when she answered the phone, was low and breathy, and when she recognized his voice, almost too expectant. Don't expect, he wanted to say to her but he didn't. He asked her to come to see him the next day in the office. It would be easier in the office. She would know what he was going to say. How could she not know, if he asked her to come to the office?

But five minutes later he changed his mind. It occurred to him that she might make a scene, scream, God knows what. Then others would hear. The walls in this old building were so thin. He called her again. He asked her to come to the apartment at six.

"I was wondering why—"

"Don't wonder, no reason." He was already evading. Or perhaps protecting her for the moment. The blow would fall soon enough.

When she came to the door of his apartment, there was, to begin with, the note that had been left on this door— No, she was not going to think of it. She simply rang, and he opened the door. Yet she was still fumbling with something that she could not catch, about doors opening and closing.

She thought of his office, of coming into his office. She, the patient, any patient entered from the hallway into a waiting room. There you waited until he had finished with the patient before you. You never saw that patient. At the end of his or her session, he or she left the consulting room through a door directly into the hallway. Then he—Edmond, yes, Edmond—opened the door to the waiting room and she, the next patient, entered, her session began, and when it was over, she went out the door to the hallway, and did not, of course, see the patient waiting in the waiting room.

She stood before him now, waiting for him to speak. He looked not impassive but severe. She wondered if was he going to say something about the letter she wrote, that she had once again gone too far. So then, what if she had gone too far? She tried to summon up the sense of exaltation that justified her writing what she did.

When his words finally came, he said she was looking well.

"Thanks," she said, and laughed a little.

"I like your dress. Is it new?"

"No, not really." She felt herself smile in a strange, newly mysterious way.

He asked her if he could get her a drink. She said yes. She sat on the couch, almost primly. He got a drink for her and one for himself. He handed her the drink and she set it before her on the coffee table.

He told her he had just been playing a record. It was Elaine May and Mike Nichols, doing a series of routines, a conversation between a young man and his mother, a young man in a car with a girl. . . .

Did she know it? No, she didn't know it.

"I'll play you just one section," he said.

He picked the one with "To think that Bartok lived on Central Park West. . . ."

They both laughed. He turned off the record. He asked her if she wanted another drink. "I'm still working on this one," she said.

He went into the kitchen to refresh his own glass. As he mixed it, he prepared himself to say to her what he had to say, simply. But how was he going to do it, now that he had started off with this skewed beginning? Unintentionally? Intentionally?

He sat down beside her on the couch, and as soon as he was seated he realized it was not a good place for him to say what he had to say. He needed some distance. He needed to be apart from her. She on the couch, he in a chair. He was about to get up but she had turned to him, was touching him, his shoulder, caressingly.

"Is it necessary to make love every time we meet?" He had tried to say it lightly. He pulled away.

He could see she was stunned.

He could see she was trying to recover. "No, of course not, not every time . . . only . . ."

"I am not a sexual athlete."

It came out suddenly. We're into harsh words now, he thought, against myself as well as her. But they are needed, the occasion demands harshness, not softness.

In his mind a strange overlapping was taking place, as if his life were nothing but a series of repetitions, first one woman, then another, then another, all of them demanding: Jean, Carol, she, she, Carol, Jean. They are asking too much of me, demanding love, understanding, that I see them, only them, when I have neither love nor understanding to give.

Yet, looking at her as she sat on his couch, he could not help but see signs of anxiety in her—a paleness, a shallow breathing, almost a shrinking. And now there began to arise in him his own anxiety, mirroring hers? tied to hers? indistinct from hers? about to take him over, as months ago, was it after that terrific fight with Jean? he could not remember, he was not sure, but whatever started it off, it had so disabled him, it paralyzed him, it threatened to overwhelm him . . . and he ended up in the hospital for two days—

"Perhaps I am wrong about that—about the demanding," he said, seeking to calm her anxiety and his own.

"I'm not demanding anything. I just wanted to—"

"Listen—" He was standing up. He was armoring himself. He held himself erect. He knew he could rely on his physical bearing, a way of holding himself, his natural authority, it was always there, no matter what.

"We have to end it, end this, what we have been doing."

He waited, dreading the breaking out in her of refusal. It was possible she would say, No, we cannot end it now.

Instead, she stared at him, silently, her dark eyes glazed, inward turning.

He said, more gently now, in explanation, in justification, that his wife was coming back earlier than expected. He was going to try to work it out with her, to make things work. So she could see that it must end now between them. He was almost gagging on the words, the lie.

She just kept looking at him. He told himself, She is holding on, he could feel her holding on to him, but she must let go.

He went into the kitchen. No hysterics yet, thank God.

She watched him go. It was as if an entire structure were giving way. I have understood nothing, she told herself, nothing at all. Still she was balancing, barely, as if on a high wire. She saw him come back into the room with a new drink in his hand. She was remembering seeing on a table in that "museum" a twisted chain, and entangled in it was a bent hook and a fragment of red material.

Seeing her stare at him, he felt, Let her count, if she wants to. This was coming to an end now, what he never should have started. She was not to blame for his being here with her. He was not forced into it, but still at the time he agreed, it did not feel as much a choice as an inevitability. This will end soon, he counseled himself, grateful for the alcohol, which suspended him above knowing or beneath it, he could not tell, he would not inquire.

Questions of knowing came to her, like a choice, like a way of fortifying herself against pain, of absenting herself from this place, this happening, for an instant. What can you know about anyone you have known for a long time? a short time? How many different kinds of knowing are there? She had thought she knew him. She did not know him. Yet in some way she did know him, not in words perhaps, perhaps not even in facts, but somehow she knew him. . . .

They were locked in an embrace, he and she, tighter than either had ever known, but false, false, he told himself, a delusion he must somehow break.

This will kill me, he thought. End it. End it.

He seized on the power of simple motion, the effect of physically turning away. He went over to the record player, he took the record off the turntable, he put the record into the inner paper sleeve, and then into the outer cardboard cover. His hands were steady, he was surprised at how steady his hands were.

When he turned to look at her, she was still sitting. Her head was bent. Into his mind flashed the image of a catatonic patient at the state hospital, where he did his residency. A young woman sitting in a chair, her shoulders turned in, her chest caved in, her legs, her knees, her ankles turned inward, her head bowed. She never spoke a word.

She said, "To stop this way would be to say it was all for nothing."

If it would only have been for nothing, he said to himself. He should have been more gentle, but how could he have been, when what was being done was by its very nature not gentle, was like tearing, like being torn.

She got up. She picked up her purse from the coffee table. She took a step toward the door then hesitated. "I may need help—if you—can you give me the name of another doctor if I need help."

He got a piece of paper from the telephone pad. He wrote down three names. He pulled out the telephone book and found the numbers. He wrote the numbers down. He handed the paper to her. "Here are three names. They are all good men—any one of them will—you can call and tell them I referred you."

He cringed at the thought of these men, his colleagues, knowing what he had done, judging what he had done. For what? he could hear them saying. For sex?

Was it for sex?

She put the paper in her purse, and then, not knowing what to say, she left.

She was in her car, turning left on Middlefield Road, going past the Children's Center, past the Library, right on Charleston, left on Nelson, just as she had after she had seen the note, after getting into his bed—only now it was not yet night, there were no dense shadows to hide in.

After she closed the door, he told himself, She will get over it. For a while she may be angry, bitter, unforgiving, but then I don't give a damn whether she forgives me or whether she doesn't. Maybe she'll be better off if she doesn't.

All I want is to be out of it.

He had another drink, and another.

At last he reached the point where he was as if becalmed in a sea, no wind, no waves, just the gentle lapping of wide water. You have been making too much of this, he told himself. He had made a mistake. He never should have done what he did, acting out as he did. But that was over now. Think of others who have done this: their patients survived, they survived. Ferenczi, Jung, God knows who else in those early days, and how many now? You made a slip, an error in judgment. It's over. It was over for them, it will be over for you. You go on to the next thing.

As if it's been wiped out. As if it's never been.

When the phone rang, he thought, I'm not going to answer it. What the hell does she want from me now? What more is there to say?

What she said about love in her letter, it's a delusion, this had nothing to do with love. It never was love. It might have been love if the circumstances were different, but the circumstances weren't different.

The phone stopped ringing, and then, after a while, started ringing again. At last he picked it up. "Yes?" he said angrily.

A man's voice was on the line. An indistinct voice, a voice with a twang. He couldn't quite make out what was being said. "You've got the wrong number," he said.

He was about to hang up.

"It's me, Vern."

"Vern?"

"Vern Gosling. Don't you remember I drove you . . ."

Now he remembered. That man from the Gold Country. The woodcutter. Who lived a peaceful life, who panned for gold.

"How did you get this number?"

"You gave it to me. Remember you said you'd like to come sometime to go gold panning? Things are looking good for next week and I thought it'd be a good time to call you, for you to come up."

"No, I can't do that."

"How about the week after?"

"No, I can't do that, either."

"I realize you're a very busy man with your medical work and all. But it could be that things will change, and you'll see your way clear to driving up just for a few days, it wouldn't have to be the whole week."

"No, I don't think so, I'm sorry."

"Well then, I could just call you another time, later, maybe during the hunting season, just sort of check in, you might change your mind."

"The way things are now, I don't think so."

"But there wouldn't be no harm in just calling, would there be?"

Why the hell couldn't the man take no for an answer? "I'll tell you what. Don't call me, I'll call you."

Later in the night, waking from fitful dreams, he wondered what would have happened if she had not taken no for an answer.

14

SHE IS COMBING HER HAIR, WHICH IS SUDDENLY THINNING. She notices dark reddish brown spots on her scalp. She looks more closely and sees they are encrusted. She is frightened and tears one off. It leaves a hole in her scalp. Underneath she can see pink brain tissue, tissue that should be buried far below the surface.

She must get to a doctor right away.

She is in an office. Edmond is there. He is singing. How curious and out of character, she thinks. He gets on roller skates and skates down and up a very steep curved hill. She thinks how she admires him for doing things she cannot do. A woman in the office says, "I guess he wasn't getting very much pleasure out of this. I hope it changes soon."

I will not interpret, she told herself when she awakened. Where has interpreting led me?

She got out of bed. She went to the bathroom. She looked in the mirror. Her hair was not thinning, she had no pustules on her scalp. No mark is left on her. No mark of suffering. The idea of suffering is not appropriate here. What has happened is false, imitative, having grown out of false love, false seeing. It happened because you wanted to go further. Well, now you have gone further. Is this what you thought it would be?

I don't know what I thought it would be.

She went into Julie's room. She was sleeping, her mouth slightly open. She stirred and made a sound. Dreams in her as well. My child, myself. My child, not myself. She, safe in bed, needs safety. I must keep her out of the reach of my own dread. A child does not deserve dread. (And she, what does she deserve? She is not sure what deserving is, anymore.)

Unable to sleep, she roamed through the house. In the dark she walked into the living room. She hit her shin against the corner of the coffee table, and gasped. How could she not have known where it is? Everything is in place, as it has been.

Nothing is as it has been.

This is not an old anguish, but rather something entirely new, as if she is now being instructed in anguish, being informed that what was before was only preparation for this, was only a pale shadow of this. So that as she moves from room to room, anguish is there in place— yes, anguish so eerily at ease with place—greeting her, teaching her its new form, having enlisted ordinary objects in its service—glasses, plates, pots, pans, pillows, blankets, toothbrushes and even the reel-to-reel tape recorder left by Michael, one of his many things he left that she does not know what to do with. . . .

She turned on the light, she went to her desk, she saw the pile of bills. She sat down to do her accounts, checked the bank statement, the deposit of $400 that Michael was sending each month, would send for a year.

Four hundred dollars a month. On the other side of the ledger $143 for the house payment, including insurance and taxes. Telephone, utilities, food, clothing—medical care was still covered under his company's plan—she went over the figures, balancing them, seeking in that balance the reassurance that things would go on, that she would go on.

And here was the application, the application she had neglected to send in, which was due by next week, the application to the state college for admission in the fall to work on getting a teaching credential. She had started to fill it out but stopped when asked for the detail of her previous education. Now she has an answer of sorts.

My previous education: I went to him for three years, three times a week. In that time I learned the rational explanations for my own irrationality. And finally I thought, I am better, no longer at the mercy of events and my own fears, able to separate myself from Michael, from my irrational marriage to Michael. And then to prove I was better, I took that risk— But now I have been rejected, dismissed, given an F for failure, he would never call it that, but the hell with what he would call it, I can call it that. I have failed, been failed.

Where is that transcendence you were so proud of, so pleased with yourself about? At this very desk, after you went to the ocean that day, you felt a sudden, even oceanic transcendence that beguiled you into words—I accept what you said—but can't we—for the time that we have—be decent to one another—we must. . . .

Inappropriate words for an application. And how about the words, "I told you I'd fuck you . . ."?

Also inappropriate. And obsolete.

It was no longer a matter of "we must" but "I must." I must recover my daily life.

Which is what she tried to do, the next day, and the next, and the next after that. Trying to pay attention to minute detail, as if the more minute it was, the more crucial: Pick up this sweater, throw out that paper, dust this table, wash that towel. . . . She must knit it—the daily life—together, weave it together, a woman's work. Yet the more she tried, the more she failed, and had to try again.

It was as if part of her unraveled the stitches the moment she knit them, pulled out the threads the moment she wove them. She was like Penelope, who daily kept weaving and unweaving to put off her suitors—but like a pathetic Penelope who had no suitor to put off.

Maybe there had always been these great holes, even abysses, between one moment and the next for her. Maybe she had once thought that by taking on this daily role, woman in the house, wife in the house, she could learn to be like others, or at least what she thought was like others. Why didn't she see she was not qualified for it?

What was she qualified for?

Anxiety—as always—anxiety.

Curse and redeemer, in its own way—when it comes, it shunts her aside, it is the new inhabitant, superseding—body no longer hers but belonging to it, obeying it—responding to it as it orders body to respond. Trembling, vacant, occupied.

Dr. Craig was a conventional-looking man who wore thick glasses and a bow tie. His weight seemed to have fallen into his lower body, causing him to lean forward a little when he walked. What did she care what he looked like? Looks, appearance, the role of the eyes in seduction and self-seduction have brought her to this pass.

When she began to tell him her story, slowly, haltingly, she sensed in him aversion, no, not as strong as that, something in him that was affronted by what had happened between her and Edmond. She saw that he saw her as wounded—but she also saw that he saw in her something that was, if not dangerous, aggressive. Yet he agreed to work with her. Perhaps he was forcing himself not to judge her. That did not matter. Nor did it matter that in some way she sensed that she was strange, even foreign to him. She had become an adept at strangeness. He will help me, she thought. He is that kind of a man, I can see that.

He did not insist on the Freudian forms of authority. She sat in a chair and faced him, no lying on a couch in this consulting room.

Each time she was about to see him she prepared herself for what she would say. She knew that was not what she was supposed to do. Before—when she worked with Edmond—there were long silences, fragments never cohering. Now she had found story, and she put it forward, presented it to be heard, a framed, made story, as if the only and final result of all that happened was to enable story to be told.

She was the audience for this telling as well. Hers was not simply the active force, recalling. She was also the receiver, receiving what memory allocated. Now this, now that.

The beginning was almost too simple. The first time she saw him, he was coming out of the old two-story building converted to offices. She was across the street, about to cross, to enter the building. She was early. It was her first appointment. She did not know what the analyst she was supposed to see looked like, but she saw him—

this man—stride down the path from the door, then make a left turn onto the sidewalk going to the main street. He did not see her, as she crossed. . . .

As for an ending that was even simpler: The last time she saw him, he said, "I am not a sexual athlete." He wrote out the names of three doctors. (Craig was one of them, the only one who had time to see her.) He said, "Tell them that I referred you."

I am a referral, I have been referred, she thought, and was referred back to what happened between the first and the last time. After the first time there was a long succession of many times in one room, all now merged into a dense, almost impenetrable haze. And then came a leap, a fracturing—and then a series of disparate incidents . . . in the car with him . . . in the cabin with him. . . .

In Craig's office she attended to the sound of this telling, retelling, as if she was in a deserted landscape and this was the only sign of life. At times she held her breath and stopped and then—and then nothing.

She began to notice, particularly when she was still, shifts in her musculature, loosenings and tightenings, announcements of a sort, that seemed to be trying to explain, to prove what words, at least her words, couldn't tell.

One night she dreamed she was a being with paper legs made up of horizontal folds, accordion-like. On another night she dreamed her right arm was lifted, and then suddenly pulled out of her shoulder, even as her left arm was pulled in the opposite direction. She struggled from sleep, only to be plunged into some rudimentary beginning, where she must learn what it is for an "I" to turn, to take a step.

Was all of this only more evidence of hysteria?

Am I still a hysteric?

Was I ever one, or was that only a name, a word, for something far more complex than a catalogue of symptoms?

She spoke to Craig of the shifts and changes within her, and of the dreams about her body. He listened, without seeming to judge. He said something about primary processes, about anxiety. She said, Yes, but it's more than that. After a silence, he added, There has been some work done on body image. He mentioned Felix Deutsch, Paul Schilder, Alexander Lowen, Wilhelm Reich. She left his office, she went out into the street, she saw others moving—walking, crossing, turning, bending—and their movements were like voices threatening to erupt within her, which must be held down so she could speak in a single voice.

She went to the library. She sought out articles, books, written by those Craig had mentioned. She started reading, she started copying words that were not her words. It was a way of gaining objectivity. It was a sustaining action, a translation from another's language on the page of the other's book, through her hand, her writing, to a language on the page of her own book.

"By restraining the muscular expression of a feeling, we can disassociate it into a motor action and a sensory feeling component. One cannot become aware of the tender feelings, if one immediately acts out every impulse, for the ego is then dominated by the physical action and its consequences. . . ."

"The body of an individual is his most immediate reality as it is also the bridge which connects his inner reality with the material reality of the outer world. . . ."

"Every sense perception is at first only a signal of the body's awareness. Originally, all were perceived as if they came from within; subject and object are one and the same. Therefore, the body is the only existing reality. . . ."

The words were not hers but they promised a link to something arising in her. They would take her where she was going. She subjected herself to these words, moving from momentary belief to momentary belief, as if they were different forms to be encountered sequentially.

To copy is to consider, and to put off considering.

It is perhaps a way of taming words.

It occurred to her that she could call him at the office, he would call her back, she would tell him she was going to Craig. He would say, Craig is a good man. That was all. There would be no other words. Yet there was the image of him, sitting in that office, he on the chair behind the patient on the couch.

And once again she was imprisoned in an idea, an image, a presentation of authority, this thing she had granted to him, handed over to him.

How she hated this in herself, this flawed rebelliousness. A world of giants, and she small. She had connived with that thought, that image. She had given over authority to him and in him saw it sicken.

She went back to the library. In the collected papers of Freud she found articles on transference, including one warning against sexual intimacy between the psychoanalyst and the patient. The words were like a harsh and irreversible sentencing: such a relationship would be a complete disaster for the treatment, the patient could never be cured thereafter.

She did not want to believe the words, she dreaded believing the words. She set the text aside. It does not apply to me, she told herself.

But the words stayed in her brain, incised, a curse.

CHAPTER

⌍ 15 ⌏

A LETTER CAME FROM MICHAEL, ENCLOSING A LETTER FROM the insurance company, saying that as a result of the change in her marital status, coverage of her condition, "Anxiety Hysteria," would be terminated.

Even if going to Craig had not solved anything—what could be solved?—it had sustained her these past weeks, months, kept her going by allowing her to tell her story, prepared or not. I have come to depend on that, on him, no matter what Freud said. But if I haven't the money to pay him—and I know Michael doesn't have the money—what am I going to do?

It is his fault, she raged, his fault that I need help but now I can't get help.

In her rage, he seemed a mammoth distant figure, living his life, having his pleasure with this one, that one, but I—I— She could almost choke on her rage.

She told Craig about the letter. She said, I am not going to let this happen to me. She said, I am going to go to Nielsen—now she was using his last name—and tell him if he doesn't help me out, I will report him to the authorities.

Craig cautioned her to wait. For the first time, he was advising her directly.

"I don't think it would be helpful to you. Think it over," he said, "before you decide."

But she would not think it over.

It is noon. He has said to come at noon. She stands at the threshold, she has rung the doorbell, she is waiting for him to come to the door, the door on which the note from Carol was pinned. So he is still living here. Where had she expected him to be living? With his wife, returned to his wife. But when she called him at the office, and said she had to see him, he said to come here.

She must remember why she is here.

She has a purpose, a point, to tell him of her need, to ask him, to demand from him, for he has some responsibility in this. No, she will not start out this way, aggressive, assertive, threatening, she will explain her situation.

When he opens the door, it is like a blow to her. She knows him. She doesn't know him. Once again she is back to the tyranny of eyes. As if her body has become nothing but eyes, and she is an insect with bulging eyes, no longer capable of motion, one whose body is inert, impaled. Even as she struggles to see him as he is, what he is, she is seeing him looking at her looking at him. . . .

He is standing ramrod straight, austere and aloof. He is resolved not to give in to desire or anything approximating desire, even pity, even justice, she sees.

He motions to her to come in. He is asking her what she needed to see him about. He speaks in his professional voice, kindly, dispassionately. She takes it as negation, negation of all that they have been through together. As if it's all been dismissed, as if it never happened, as if she's never been here before. She will not conspire with him in that.

"I see you are still living here."

"Where did you expect me to be?" Yes, now his voice is different, no longer so professional. His face is different too, the muscles around his jaw tensed. What was that question he asked her when she told him about the howling? Did I bare my teeth?

"I thought by now you would be back ..."

"Back?"

"Back with your wife."

"It didn't work out, our—our reconciliation." He shrugs. "Do you want a drink?"

She shakes her head no. He goes over to the bar and pours himself a Scotch. He gestures to the couch. "Won't you sit down?"

"I'd rather stand."

"Suit yourself."

After a pause, he adds, "You said on the phone that you had something to say to me that couldn't wait."

She is not yet ready to say what she has to say. There has to be preparation. She blurts out that she is going to Dr. Craig—

"He is a good man."

That she has expected these words from him does not make it any easier for her to go on. "That is I—I—," and here she stumbles, "I have been going to him up to now but now that Michael and I are being divorced, I will no longer be able to go to him. The insurance which paid for it was from Michael's job, but once there is a divorce, the company will no longer pay. I have come to—"

To ask for help, financial help, to keep on going for treatment.

Freud said in cases like hers, yes, she is a case, it will do no good—but she does not know what else to do. It seems her only hope for survival. She will ask him for help, for a few months, to get through this time, though asking him is an agony. For isn't he responsible? Yes, responsible. His is the stated responsibility, he as doctor, she as patient. But it is more complex than that, there are multiple responsibilities, she knows, hers as well as his, each vying against the other, claiming need and exemption.

Even as she is saying what she has to say, she is shunting her own words aside. Her thoughts keep slipping into other thoughts. Not free association, there is nothing free in any of this. Everything has to be paid for, not only once but over and over again. . . .

So now in this room, it has come to this—she is standing before him, asking for payment of a kind, compensation of a kind. Otherwise—she will not say this but surely he knows that she can tell some professional board what he has done, if he does not help her. His face is a mask, lapidary, almost indifferent. As if he didn't give a damn if she reported him, as if in fact he is taunting her to do it. . . .

He goes to get another drink. He says, "I'll think about it. I'll let you know."

"I need to know—soon."

"I'll let you know in a few days."

"You said on the phone that you would be away starting tomorrow."

"That's true. I'll call you the week after."

She sees a suitcase standing near the doorway. She has noticed it when she first came in, but it is as if she has put off noticing. "So you are going away?"

"Yes."

She must force him out of hiding. "Where are you going?"

"To Mexico."

She thinks of the trip with him to Mexico that she might have taken, but did not take. And now he is about to go to Mexico, indulging himself and whoever he is taking with him, Carol, probably Carol, while all the indulging she can do is in memory, and clotted memory at that.

"I'm going there to get a divorce," he says.

"A Mexican divorce?"

He nods. Here is more hiding, more evading.

"But is that legal?"

"Legal enough."

"Why don't you get it here?"

"It's not easy to get a divorce here. You know that."

Yes, she knows that. You have to prove fault, infidelity, desertion. You have to lie if necessary—

"And even when you get it, it doesn't become final for a year. I don't want to wait that long."

"I see," she says, though she does not quite see. "What is your hurry, after all this time?"

"I've arranged to get married," he says.

Arranged? What a coward he is, she thinks. Arranged a life of pleasure for him—and Carol—while I—

Rage breaks through, she cannot stem it, she doesn't want to stem it, only to ride it. "You used to talk of facing things—you who are always escaping. Pleasure. That is what you want—that is all you ever wanted.

"I curse you—" she cries out. Words like stones cast at him, words like pieces of flesh torn from her. This is no time for thought, only for saying, for moving. "I curse you for the rest of your life—for what you have done—for what you are doing—for your own pleasure."

"You're wrong," he says. "It is not pleasure I am after, but peace."

WHEN HE CALLED HER, A WEEK AND A HALF LATER, HE SAID, "I have decided not to do what you asked."

Did he expect another outburst? Instead she said, "It turns out that Michael's insurance is going to continue paying until the divorce decree is final, so I'm all right."

There was a brief pause, and then he said, "Incidentally, I'm married."

After she hung up, she realized it was his use of the word "incidentally" that stopped her from saying anything more.

What had happened with him had all been about words, after all. To begin with, it had been about words that were caught in her throat, so she could hardly speak. Then slowly over time there were halting words, muddled words, words that came in a rush. And while she was speaking and he was listening, belief began to grow in words as revelation, a belief in the curative power of words.

But now words that had once been freeing, curative, had turned to weapons, in her own mouth, as well as his. She had cursed him—she could not think about it without a sense of shame—and he had used that word "incidentally," implying that she was not relevant, not germane, off to the side, beside the point.

In a session with Craig, she told him—it was part of her story, a part that had been delayed up to now, for at times, she saw, there were necessary delays in telling, but now she must hurry—"Once, after sex, he said to me, 'I told you I'd fuck you, you bitch.'"

Craig, owlish behind his glasses, said, "He was thinking of his wife."

I don't think so, she thought, but did not say.

She went to the library, going back to Freud's words warning against a psychoanalyst and a patient entering into "a love-relationship which is illicit . . . made impossible by conventional morality and professional standards," advising that when confronted with such a situation with a patient, the psychoanalyst should stress to the patient the "resistance" in this "love."

"Genuine love, we say, must make her docile and intensify her readiness to solve the problems of her case simply because the man she was in love with expected it of her."

And then followed a paragraph about one particular class of women who are resistant to even such persuasion, a "class of woman with whom the attempt to preserve the erotic transference for the purpose of analytic work without satisfying it will not succeed. These are women of elemental passionateness who tolerate no surrogate. They are children of nature who refuse to accept the psychical in place of the material, who, in the poet's words, are accessible only to 'the logic of soup, with dumplings for arguments.'"

CHAPTER

ᗢ 17 ᗡ

IN THE MIDDLE OF THE NIGHT SHE AWOKE TO A SOUND.
She turned on the light. Someone was in the room. It was Julie, staring, unseeing, making the sound, a low, guttural gagging.

"What's the matter?" she cried out.

The child did not answer. Her face, so delicately featured, was
stony, taut.

Jumping out of bed, she moved to her, to embrace her, to hold her
tight.

"Don't touch me!" she cried.

She dropped her hands. She stood facing her, uncertain as to what
to do.

"It's all right," she said. "It's okay. You're having a dream, a nightmare. Here, let me—" She put out her hand to her.

Again the child shrank back.

"Don't touch me."

They stood, facing each other, like opponents.

"Let me," she said, and moved forward to enclose her in her arms, but even as she did so, even as the child softened and began to moan, she felt she had committed a transgression, had violated something, a boundary.

Julie was shivering.

"Come into the bathroom," she said. "You can take a warm bath."

The child nodded her head. She held her close as she turned on the water, took off her nightgown and put her in the tub. She was silent in the tub, unmoving. But soon her eyes were no longer staring. They were coming back to seeing, as if she was coming back.

"Do you want to come out now?"

Yes, she nodded.

"Are you ready to go to bed?"

She nodded again.

She dressed her, she took her back to bed. She covered her. "Are you warm enough?"

Yes, the child nodded, and was instantly asleep.

She sat beside the bed for a long time, watching.

In the morning, Julie showed no sign of remembering the night before.

She waited in Craig's waiting room, while he talked to the child. When Julie came out with him, at the end of the session, she gave no sign of anything having happened. She only said, when they got out the door, "You said we could go and get ice cream sodas at Blum's."

"Yes, that's where we're going."

Later, in the ice cream shop, she said to her, "Do you want to tell me anything about your—your visit?"

"It was okay. We played Uncle Wiggly."

"Did you talk?"

"A little. He asked me some questions. I don't want to go again. It was boring."

When she told Craig, he said that perhaps the night terror was only a single incident. "Wait and see how she does."

She waited and in fact the night terror did not recur. But she could not rid herself of the recurring shock of hearing Julie cry out in that strange voice, "Don't touch me."

She thought of how it was when she discovered she was pregnant with her: she and Michael had been trying for a long time with no luck, and then she had had a period as usual, but slight, slight bleeding, which was unusual for her, and then, following that had even another period, even slighter bleeding, but still— She had gone to the gynecologist for a checkup, her abdomen was no longer flat and she told him she thought she might have a growth. You have a growth all right, he'd said.

And she remembered that afterward she had gone to sit in a café, on a second story, looking out toward the hills—and the sunlight kept bounding and rebounding off of everything, buildings, cars, the hills—the light convincing her that with this new life within her, her own life would change irrevocably, for the better.

So she had felt, so she had been convinced, and so it had seemed— but how was it that specters interfered, anxiety, for instance, yes, a large for instance—you let them filter in, ruin, destroy—

She had thought she was keeping her child safe, sealing her off from being contaminated by her own anxiety, but all she had managed to do was to become an even greater conduit of it to her. How long had this been happening to the child and how long had she not seen it? It is, she suddenly thought, as if I am the one who has been sealed off, from her and from my own history.

It was one thing to choose to take a risk, and in so doing to damage yourself. It was another to damage your child who has been entrusted to you, who has no choice in the matter. If necessary, and it now seemed necessary, she would become ruthless with herself, would insist on attention to what is, not on what could or might be. If and when anxiety came back again, let it come, with all its rawness and its deception. And damn the deceiver, she would take Equanil if she had to. She hated taking it, it slowed her down, clogged her brain, but she would take it, when and if anxiety came.

Here was daytime—daytime, thank God, her newfound ally after too much darkness, lending its light to habit, to detail, to each single moment, to any and every specific moment—to helping Julie put on the green cotton dress with ruching on the bodice that she had picked out herself—for she only wanted to wear dresses now—to giving her breakfast—she did not like breakfast—Cheerios, milk, most of it left, she will not insist that she finish it, and she walked her down the street to the light on Charleston, and then watched her cross under the eye of the crossing guard, and she was off and running with the other chidren into the school yard—and then she walked home, went into the house, dressed, and got in the car, a white station wagon, a Ford, with an automatic transmission that suddenly had this thing wrong with it—when you went up or down a hill, it slipped out of gear, the mechanic had tried to fix it but couldn't, and she drove to the state college where she was taking a class in education, and an elementary class in psychology,

Human Development, it was the only one that was available in the morning. . . .

Since this is the first class of the semester, the instructor was saying, I'd like you to write something about yourself, so I can get to know you a little before we start. A student raised her hand. What kind of thing do you mean? Well, for example, said the instructor, write about an important incident in your life, and what you learned from it.

In the seat next to her a young woman has printed her name at the top of the paper, Sandy Burke. Around the room others are writing, their heads bent over their work. The instructor, a tall, efficient-looking woman, is making an entry in a large black notebook.

Her own paper is blank. Not even her name is on it.

An important incident. Incidentally, an incident.

She glances again at the paper of Sandy Burke. "In my last year of high school," she has written, "I wanted to be the student council representative for my class. I worked very hard and I made posters and I talked to my friends. But when the election came, I wasn't picked. After a while, I got over it. I learned that we all have to be loosers sometime."

She has a sudden and vicious urge to laugh.

It's not funny, she accuses herself. It happens to be true. Other people can learn from life, why can't you? You have a basic flaw in your vision, an incapacity to see what any normal person can see, a normal person like Sandy Burke, even if there's a flaw in her spelling.

"Five more minutes," the instructor says.

She starts to write, "When I—"

She crosses it out.

All the incidents of her past from childhood on have been tainted by telling.

"Two more minutes."

She is thinking that even now, when she drives past where Edmond lives, past the single street that is a dead end, there erupts in her a longing so intense. . . .

There is nothing to be learned from that.

"Pass your papers up to the front."

She is thinking of that road like a corridor that led to a mine shaft they never reached because the car broke down. She is thinking if they would have reached the mine shaft, and walked too close to the edge of it, if the ground had given way beneath their feet, if they both fell into the shaft, hurtling down past ledges on either side, from which stared faces, eyes watching them. . . .

There is certainly nothing to be learned from that.

CHAPTER

18

THE LANDSCAPE WAS BARREN, TOTALLY FLAT, NO MOUND OR declivity anywhere, until suddenly they came to a canyon, they could see it below them, a stream snaking through it. There, said Vern, that's where we'll find it. They slid down the steep incline, hurtling past loose rock. At the bottom the stream had dried out to no more than a trickle. This place is no good, we won't find anything, Vern shook his head. Then why did you bring us here? he yelled. With those steep walls on either side, we'll never get back. You have to fly up, Vern said, and in an instant he was gone. But there was no way he could fly, he kept trying to climb, desperately jumping at the crumbling rock, looking for a handhold, his hands rough and bleeding, he would never get out, he tried to cry for help, but no sound came.

He awoke in a sweat, his pulse pounding. Carol was shaking him. "What? What?" he said.

"You were having a nightmare," she said. "You're still shaking."

"It's okay. I'm all right," he said.

He had just finished with his last appointment when he heard a knock on the door to the outside hallway. Ann Hollister, it was undoubtedly her. She was always forgetting something. Her watch, her scarf, she'd left it on the couch. Another excuse to come back. He opened the door to the hallway. It was not Hollister, it was Lee Adams.

Right off Adams was smiling, smiling but accusing. "I left a message with your service but you didn't call back."

"I've been busy."

"It's not like you not to call back. You always call back, I know," and here Adams smiled his crooked smile.

"I said I've been busy."

"Expecting anyone else?"

"No, I'm done for the day."

"How about going out for a drink?"

"No, I don't think so. I've got to be getting home."

"Mind if I come in for a minute? It'll just take a minute." Stepping inside, he looked around the office. "So," he said, "I heard you got married. That is, divorced and remarried."

"That's usually the sequence."

Adams grinned, as if he was determined not to be offended. "Fast worker."

"So it seems."

"Not that I blame you. Once you cut the cord, it's best to strike when the iron is hot. Sorry," he grinned again, "I seem to be mixing metaphors these days. Oh, I brought you a present. A little wedding present." He pulled a small package out of his pocket and handed it to him.

Inside was a small wood carving of a human figure with a fierce face, masklike but smiling; it had many arms.

"It's something I picked up when we were traveling in India. It's supposed to bring good luck, and all that, to the new household."

"Well, it's very nice and I thank you but it wasn't necessary to—"

Abruptly, Adams sat down on the couch and leaned forward. He was a tall thin man in his late fifties, impeccably dressed, his dark hair turning to gray, handsome except for something in the expression of his face, even more pronounced at this moment, something shifty or needy.

"Good marriage? Things going well?"

"Yes."

"The first full flush of romance?"

He didn't answer.

"I was surprised when I heard about the divorce. You always seemed so happy with Jean."

He almost laughed at this. "Did I?"

"Well, appearances. Well, actually, I can't say I'm sorry you got rid of her. A stunner, no doubt, but she was a witch."

He shrugged. "I don't know where you got that idea."

"Oh, come on, it didn't take a genius to see what was going on. The way she was always trying to tear you down in front of other people. . . ."

"Why do you say that?"

"I saw it all the time at our parties. Must have made you feel lower than shit, but you never even gave a sign of it."

After a silence Edmond said, "Jean had her troubles."

"Don't we all?"

"She had an unhappy childhood."

"Didn't we all?"

"Look, I'm divorced. I'm remarried, everything's fine. Jean and I came to an agreement."

"It must have been nasty."

Yes, it was nasty, and still was being nasty, but he didn't have to say that to Adams. He looked at his watch. "I do have to go. But thanks for stopping by and thanks for the present."

Adams kept sitting there, staring at him. "Is something the matter?" he asked.

"Why should anything be the matter? I'm married, I mean, I'm remarried—"

"You look different—edgy, as if you're about to explode at any second. Did something happen?"

"Nothing happened."

"Objectively speaking . . ."

"You, objective?"

"Yes, objectively—" Adams was saying. "How long have we known each other? Ten years? I've never seen you like this. Maybe you've got too many patients. Maybe you should ease off."

"My patient load isn't any heavier than it ever was," he said irritably.

"Maybe it's the kind of patients you take on. You were always one to take on the most intransigent cases. Like you had to prove something."

"Lee, I don't need any of this, least of all from you. So if you don't mind—"

"I just want to say one thing. I get the feeling that you're burned out, and it's not surprising. I remember the way you were when you started your practice, so eager, too eager, so diligent, so devoted to your patients. No one could keep that up forever."

He didn't want to think about how he had been. "Could we end this discussion?"

"It's not a discussion. I'm simply talking about all of this." He waved his hand. "The office. The sitting in the chair behind the couch. The evenly suspended attention, the silence, the hours and hours you spend listening, four times a week you're listening to them, they're going on and on with their complaints, wanting you to rescue them, wanting you to sleep with them, wanting you to make your profound pronouncements, profound, oh, deeply profound. . . . For some people this is good. For some people, but not for you."

"It never was, for you, in case you've forgotten."

"It's true. That's why I gave up my practice—"

"Or it gave you up."

"Possibly," he laughed. "In any case, I never regretted it for one minute. I find research much more rewarding."

"Glad to hear that. Now, as I said, I've got to—"

"Before I go, let me tell you—" But then, he lapsed into silence. He looked around vaguely, as if he had forgotten where he was.

"Well?"

"Well, what?"

"For Christ's sake, you said you wanted to tell me something."

"About our institute. You heard about our institute? Johnson, Grady, Tyler, and me, we finally got some funding. We're doing some experiments with volunteers taking LSD. I tell you, I'm taking it myself, and once you've done it, you can really see—you have to experience it to know what I'm talking about. All this other stuff pales beside it," and again he waved his hand around the office, "the rigid rules, the rigid theoretical constructs, the couch, the free association, the years and years getting at this repressed memory and that repressed memory—"

"As I remember, you told me long ago that you don't believe in repression."

"Give me proof of repression. For that matter, give me proof of the Oedipal complex."

"I've always found it helpful with my patients."

"Listen," he said, "there are amazing truths all around us, right in front of us, if you just open your eyes."

He paused and went on slowly, as if he was picking his way through a verbal minefield. "Things are changing. Everything's changing. It's the explosion of the paradigm—"

"What the hell are you talking about, Lee?"

"That's what Johnson calls it: the explosion of the paradigm, the explosion of the old ways of thinking—in the world, about the world. Something new is coming in, it's about to replace them. How we think about things. How we feel about things. There were signs before this, if you were smart enough to catch them. You could see it in the way the superego was already on the way out. I saw this in my patients, years ago."

"Ah, so the superego is out." He was determined to respond patiently, calmly.

"Just think about it for a minute. How can it not be? I mean, Freud was making his discoveries fifty years ago, and who were his patients? Upper-middle-class women hysterics in Vienna. Maybe it worked for them, but for now—"

"Lee, you know we're constantly discussing changes in the way we approach—"

"You think those rigid authoritarian bastards in charge are going to allow—"

"Lee, Lee, I have got to go—my wife is expecting me."

Adams looked at the Bokhara patterns on the rug on the floor.

He seemed to be trying to divine their significance. After a moment, he said, "You know, all that talk about the lifting of the veil of consciousness—it's not a metaphor. It's actuality. I can tell you don't believe me but—"

"Well, I'm sure you—"

"I tell you, it's true. I was up in the city last week. I was in Union Square. I sat down on a bench. And all of a sudden this feeling came over me—it had been two weeks since I'd taken LSD—but it was the feeling coming back, the veil of consciousness was lifting, and I was seeing—I saw how the buildings were beginning to lean, lean inward, toward me, all those buildings around the square, the St. Francis Hotel, and I. Magnin's, all of them, they were leaning inward toward me. I knew, of course I knew they were still standing straight and solid, but I also knew they were leaning in toward me. I could still see and hear everything that was going on around me, it wasn't like I was caught in a dream, I could see the people walking, the pigeons eating their corn on the sidewalk, and flying up when someone came too near, I could hear their sound, and the sound of the traffic, it was all going on, but at the same time, I had broken through to that other time and space, I could see in the way those buildings were leaning. . . . I'm not talking about some inner space here, but an equivalent, more real space, neither out nor in, in which things are both solid and inert and at the same time they are always moving, so all our talk about what we see as fixed—

"Take this couch." He laid his hand on it. "Take this couch," he repeated, and then abruptly shook his head. "No, don't take this couch."

He was silent for a moment and then he stood up and smiled his crookedly seductive smile. "Does she have a name?"

"Who?"

"Your wife, your new wife, your second wife."

"Carol, her name's Carol."

"Nice name," he said and grinned. "Say hello to Carol for me."

At the door, he turned. "I can see you don't believe me, but think about it, it could transform your life if you could once allow yourself to take a little trip out of your own unregenerate version of reality."

Adams was always unstable, he told himself. But this time, the drug could have thrown him into psychosis. And if it has? There's not a goddam thing I can do about it. He would never listen to me. He was always an intellectual gadfly, always latching on to the newest fad, brilliant in his way, but it was one of those quick brilliances, he became bored, things became tedious, he had to move on to the next thing. Several times in years past Adams had buttonholed him after meetings and tried to convert him to his latest enthusiasm. Who was it the last time? Wilfred Bion.

He'd tried to fend Adams off by saying, "Frankly, I'm not all that interested in theory as theory. What matters to me is therapy."

At which point, Adams had said, "Freud said theory is therapy." You never could win with him.

The superego is out? Like hell.

What am I going to do with that damned wooden carving?

He hated the face with its cruel smile. He didn't want to leave it here.

When he got to the Jaguar, he threw it on the floorboard behind the driver's seat, where it would stay for weeks, unnoticed.

CHAPTER

～ 19 ～

HE IS WALKING DOWN A STREET, HER STREET. HE HAS PARKED
a few houses away. He did not want to park in front of her house;
someone might notice, someone might see him going in. He has
told himself, It is finished, it has ended, how can it not be ended? Yet
here he is, on this street, walking toward her house, when he thought
he wanted peace.

It's not that there hasn't been peace in his married life. There has
been. Yet here he is walking down her street to her house, propelled
by what is not peace, by what has nothing to do with peace.

Weeks ago, by chance, he met her in the post office downtown.
She was wearing white shorts; he noticed her slim tanned legs. She
saw him, she greeted him; she seemed composed. He was grateful for
that composure. He told himself he was pleased she was doing well.
Yet he could not stop himself from feeling desire behind that com-

posure. He told himself, Don't see it, it's better not to see it, you can walk away from it—now. Which he did, and thought instead of peace, how he needed peace.

But afterward he kept thinking of her, wondering about that composure. Was it only acting? No, it seemed to be composure, some kind of resolution, and yet, still, the desire.

Yesterday he called her, the day after Carol left for a visit to her mother in Seattle. He said he was calling to say he had just moved into her neighborhood, two streets away. He said he wanted to let her know, he didn't want to upset her if they met by chance in the neighborhood, at the community center, at the swimming pool.

"Thank you for letting me know," she said.

And then how was it, who began it, one thing led to another, and here he is walking to her house on this sidewalk, walking by lawns and fruit trees already in bloom, though it is only February. The slanting sun is warm on his face, but he experiences a sudden chill.

He walks down the cement path that leads to her front door; it is identical to the path that leads to the front door of the house he has moved into with Carol.

At her door he stands an instant to prepare himself to see her seeing him.

He rings the doorbell. When she opens the door, he is not prepared. There seem to be two women before him, one replacing the other, alternating with the other. One woman, slender, attractive, dark-haired, greeting him. The other woman, more image than being—but no less powerful for that—someone who is like a template for him, a pattern useful for subversion, for imagining and anguish.

He should not have come here.

She smiles at him: she is not two, she is only one.

"Did you walk?" she asks, looking toward the street.

"No, I drove."

"Where's your car?"

"I left it down the street. I thought someone might see. . . ."

"No one will see," she says.

He shrugs. Easy enough for her to say.

She offers him a drink. "Scotch and soda?" He declines, he says he doesn't have much time. "I have to get back to the office by three. I have a patient at three."

After he says the word "patient," there is a long silence between them.

"My three o'clock patient is the angriest man I ever met. He has been coming to me for three years—and he is still an angry man."

By now they are sitting on the couch, he beside her. He is looking out the window into the garden. The leaves in the sunlight are still and sharply etched, laced with a blinding clarity. But within this room everything is blurred, out of focus, diffused. She cursed him, and yet he is back, even though cursed, seeking relief in what he believes is a newfound gentleness in her.

"Sometimes I wonder what good I have done him."

He is about to add, What good have I done any of them? but he does not, he must not, he has been harmful enough to her, as is.

He holds out his hand to her. If it is not a desperate movement in and of itself, it feels like desperation to him.

She takes his hand.

Now, after all that has happened, here she is with him in a strange togetherness—he has no other word for it—a togetherness in a moment of peace, wrung out of risk . . . two beings together. . . .

He feels something like relief, an easing. He says, After all, he will have a drink. She gets up and comes back with Scotch. Look, he says to himself, see, she is not demanding. I can say to her what I want to say, what I have to say, what I need to say. He can even talk of the future, of his plans for the future. And when I talk of the future, she will look at it with me, consider it with me, not take a stand against me, be on my side.

"I am thinking," he says, "of moving north."

"Now?"

"No, next year. To Seattle. Carol's family is there. She would rather be there."

"But you would have to give up your practice?"

"Yes, of course."

"And start another one there?"

"I'm not sure. I am thinking of another speciality. I am board-certified in neurology as well. I would just need to take some refresher courses."

After a pause, he adds, "And you, what are you doing?"

"I've gone back to school—"

"That's good," he says.

Suddenly she gets up. "I forgot, I have your book. The book you lent to me a long time ago." She gets up and goes over to the book-case and brings back a book.

"What did you think of it?"

"I'm not sure I remember that well." She recalls its prophetic tone.

"You know Reich was arrested, for mail fraud, put in jail."

"I didn't know."

"He died in jail. He was found dead one morning in his cell. He became quite mad at the end."

"But the book does not seem mad."

"He wrote it very early, in 1933, while he was still in Germany, before he came to the U.S. He had had some arguments with Freud, so Freud broke with him. But he had some very interesting things to say about armoring, about character armoring and muscular armoring, about how the body and the mind work together. I thought you'd be interested in it, since you spoke about such things in your own therapy."

Therapy. In her therapy with him. Between them the word has a hollow ring. She puts the book on the coffee table in front of them. It lies inert in its canvaslike cover.

He picks it up and turns to the table of contents. "He covers a lot of ground here, I've forgotten how much, it's been years since I read it. 'Some Problems of Psychoanalytic Technique,' 'On the Technique of Interpretation and Resistance Analysis,' 'Indications and Dangers of Character Analysis,' 'On Handling the Transference. . . .'"

He closes the book. "Why don't you keep it?"

"Are you sure you don't want it?"

He says, "I have no need of it anymore."

No need for it as book, but arising out of the book, because of the book, despite the book, is another need, pressing upon him like an onslaught, an unbearable excitement that is the very antithesis of peace. He knows it is madness, yet here is his body succumbing, his penis stirring to erection, and the more he tells himself he should not give in, the harder he becomes.

In her eyes he sees the reflection of his own desire.

In her bed, in her bedroom where the shadow of the roof overhang triangulates the sun on the closed cream-colored drapes, he feels himself falter, feels desire falter, his penis becoming slack. His excitement is being reabsorbed by cells that are unconvinced.

With his skin smooth against hers, she feels the faltering. She waits, she thinks, I must give him time. I have never given him enough time. But she is being pulled two ways. Longing has resurfaced in her, that fierce and irresistible impulse to throw herself with him into the unknown, the unbound, deep and dark with risk—now, this moment.

By now his penis is totally retracted. He pulls away from her. Lying on his back, staring at the wooden ceiling, he sees the dark spaces between the boards. She is embracing him, he is pulling out of the embrace. He pushes her head down, down to his penis. She must help him out.

She feels the pushing, she has seen the slackening. But why now does she feel that authority is being mimicked here, is being reinstituted by him in some way, she sees that in his gesture. Yet where is generosity? He is in need. She is touched by his need. She must help him out. For love. For what she has seen in him. For the sake of a dream fast vanishing.

Seeing her hesitation, he says, "You don't like my sex."

She does what he wants, but even so, his response is only half-hard. She is left with a quivering of her own desire. Yet there must be allowances. They are in this together, side by side now, she to his left, he to her right, he on his back, she on her stomach.

She puts her left arm around him. She leans her head on his shoulder. She smells the delicate, clear smell of his skin. No odor of liquor now, and only the faintest smell of sweat. They lie silently, for a minute. Abruptly, he says, "Sorry," and dislodges her as he leans over to the bedside table where he has left his cigarettes. He takes out a cigarette and lights it. He lies back with one hand behind his head. He turns and smiles at her gently.

"I hate the fact that you are going to Craig, telling him. . . ."

She does not know what to say. She hears in his voice a claim on her that she must resist. She is just about to terminate with Craig, in any case. Is he saying this because of what just happened? Has he been thinking I will report to Craig about his coming, about what he did and did not do? Is that why he could not perform, but what does this have to do with performance?

I had no right to say this to her, he tells himself. And yet he has said it.

"I've been thinking," he says, "when I go, when I leave my practice, I'll have to refer my patients—maybe you could . . ."

"Could what?"

"Take over one or two of them, with training, with supervision. A therapeutic analysis is not all that different from a training analysis, if you . . ."

She thinks, He's drunk, How can he be drunk on one drink? She says, "You're kidding, of course."

He thinks, No, I'm not kidding. Then he laughs, as if he were kidding.

Feeling his skin smooth against hers, she will not judge him. If they were unequal before, they are almost equal now.

"What you said earlier," she asks him, "once, at—at the climax, you said, you cried out, 'I told you I'd fuck you, you bitch.' Who were you thinking of?

He shakes his head. "Why do you ask?" he says.

Afterward is abrupt and unsettled. He dresses, she dresses, each turned away from the last moments of nakedness. Yet when she opens the door for him to leave, she is already thinking about what will happen now.

"So you may go soon," she says.

"Go where?"

"To Seattle."

"No, not soon. Not for a while."

And during this "while" if he calls her, will she agree to his coming? For all that has happened—she has seen something like disinte-
gration in him—and she is fearful for him—yet there is a reverence
in her for him—it will never, she is sure, go away, that awe—that
sense of him as a sacred being—though, she now feels, he has been
trying to destroy that image of him in her, still will she go on, will
she be waiting for him? She can see herself waiting for him, thrown
back into waiting minute by anguished minute, day by day, for his
call—how she loathes servitude, and yet how she must long for it.

"If you want to see me," she says—she does not know how to say
this—but she is determined to take a stand, to prove that this is more
than servitude. "I do not want it to be as it was before—that you call
when you want to call, after weeks, after months— If you want to see
me, it must be different. It must be clear during this time before you
go—"

"If I go—" He is looking at her, his blue eyes intent, evaluating.

"If you want to see me—in this way—so that I do not wait without knowing—let me know by Saturday. If you don't call me by
Saturday, don't call."

He smiles. An odd smile. "The one you were when you first came
to me would not have been able to say that."

She shrugs.

"So I have done you some good, after all."

He turns and walks down the path to the sidewalk. Watching him,
she sees the slight twist in his torso, as he turns and walks down the
street to where he left his car.

CHAPTER

∽ 20 ∾

HIS PATIENT HARNACK IS SAYING, SHE SAID . . . I SAID . . .
She said . . . and in the next minute he is speaking of sex with his
wife as revenge and neediness, revenge for his neediness. Words of
rage, at how he is tied to her, bound to her despite how she—

He makes himself listen, he makes himself attend to the manner
and pattern of Harnack's telling. It is old story, told how many times
over in this room at this hour, Harnack and his wife entwined in
rage, held together by rage, each having found the perfect partner to
cement their individual rages together. He does not need his notes to
remind him of the repetitions of scenes, the playing out again and
again, and yet it holds, the marriage holds.

And, of course, still, yet, the rage in the transference, though for all
he has tried to get Harnack to acknowledge it, he denies it, cloaks it
in neediness.

And now—this too part of the pattern of telling—Harnack is saying what is it within him that will not allow him to let go, to escape—yes, yes, he knows, in his own way he asks for it—yes, he admits it, he asks for it somehow, each time, he tells himself but he does not change. And then silence, and then, a shift in his bodily posture as he lies there, a sudden slumping on the couch—and then "My father—"

Oedipal, still Oedipal, his litany never changed, no matter what the interpretation, he will say, Yes, yes, will agree, Yes, that's it, but will nevertheless go on as he has.

Analysis terminable and interminable— It may be time to say simply, I can do nothing further for you. He is about to say, It's time to think of—when he catches sight of Harnack's shoeless feet on the couch, turned inward, the toes under the yellow socks leaning toward each other, almost touching, and his heart lurches in pity.

I can do nothing further for any of them.

He tells himself to stop this, he must stop this— But here now, as he is hearing Harnack say, "When I was at school . . . ," he has fallen into memory, the memory of being a boy at school, he was twelve or so, just before the Christmas holidays, the day the principal arranged for his class to go to the county poorhouse to sing carols for the "poor unfortuates" living there. The poorhouse was miles out of town, set back from the road, a large dark building in the snow, made of wood, with many eaves. Inside in a cold bare room, on folding chairs, women and children, men too, and a boy his own age, waiting. They sat in silence, slumped, as if life had discarded them into those ragged rows.

He stared at the boy, who had sandy hair and blue eyes, just like his own. He had never thought of himself as having another self until that moment. But now having thought of it, found it, he was in dan-

ger. By one slip he could fall forever into the other. He could be in
that boy's place. Yes, it could happen to him now that his father had
died, now that they had lost the store, now that they were going to
lose their house—that they—he and his mother—would have to go
to the poorhouse (though they never did) —

What did he do? He thinks he turned away. Maybe he whispered
a joke to his friend Fred, a joke about the boy's knickers falling down
to his ankles.

If pressed too far, memory simply throws up its hands. Memory
can do that, can refuse, can make itself inert, can be cannily unforgiving.

"I did not expect my life would turn out like this," Harnack is
saying.

He is walking up the path to the door of his house, the house he and
Carol are renting. It is just like the path to her house, cement with
wooden headers. Two paths to two houses in the same tract, a multi-
plying and a splitting, the same and not the same.

This door. That door.

In this house. In that house.

Alone in this house (he has almost forgotten, how could he have
forgotten, Carol will not be here, she has gone to visit her mother,
who is ill), this house that is like her house, though of course the furnishings are not the same, he pours himself a drink and sits and
drinks, and gets up and pours himself a drink and sits and drinks
again.

He knows enough to know that he must, that he can stop right
now, just as he could have stopped when he found himself walking
down the street to her house, but he didn't stop. And then once there,

after the talk, what was the talk, after the book, came the frantic desire for her.

And the consequent action—inaction—

She is not rescue to him. She never was rescue. Yet why did he think something in her promised rescue and risk at the same time, rescue by risk?

The phone rings. It is—even as he wonders at the sudden rapid beating of his heart—it is Carol.

She says, "Did I wake you up, darling? You sound tired."

"I had a hard day. But it's okay. How are you? How's your mother?"

"She's better, so I'll be coming back Friday. And you'll pick me up at the airport."

"Yes, of course."

"I miss you," she says. "I love you."

Rescue, he has been rescued.

In the morning, a new beginning. It's Wednesday, a beautiful day, infinitely promising, one of those days when the light is golden, the sky an ever-deepening blue, the air so soft, yet the edge of everything is sharp and clear. Once he is in the office, he does what he does, he is what he does. In this room where for years he has sought to help his patients, and did, yes, did—often—help them, he hears what is said and not said with a piercing clarity. And they, his patients, in turn, are moving from discovery to discovery with barely any intervention on his part, as if all of his work with them has been leading up to this.

Simultaneously, things in the room are being summoned from obscurity—his licenses framed in black, the white Venetian blinds covering the windows, the Japanese lithograph of an exotic bird that Jean put up when he moved in here, the doors, the many doors—

each thing stands out sharply, each thing in its place, as if a veil has been lifted.

When he gets home, he decides to have one drink, yes, one will be enough. He is no longer at risk. He is leading, not being led. He gets the ice tray out of the freezer unit, loosens the cubes from the tray with the metal release, puts the ice in the glass, drops the extra ice in the sink, pours new water into the ice tray, puts the tray back in the freezer, opens the bottle of Scotch, hears the sound of the pouring, the sound of the ice crackling, lifts the glass, swallows. . . .

In the early morning, he wakes suddenly, and there before him, at the foot of the bed, is a woman in brilliant plumage, yellow and blue, with black stripes, standing, silent, her eyes glittering. He cannot believe what he is seeing. In the next moment he is awake and she is gone. A hypnagogic hallucination—caught between sleeping and waking, he invented her. Or else his drinking—one drink?—invented her.

No, he will not analyze it, will not make connections to—to what? —to the bird on the wall of his office? Too easy, too easy. Nothing can be laid out so exactly, grid by grid, explanation by explanation.

In his office from his chair behind the couch, he keeps staring at the bird, an image not at all like the woman in the dream, with its long, pointed beak, a golden head, a dark red body, upper feathers that are blue and green edged with blue, long, narrow tail feathers dark red and pink, marked by scrolling, like a written message, its talons grasping a branch, poised for flight.

Yet such is the force of habit, or belief, that at the same time he is staring, he has been attending to his patients—at the moment it is Hollister—to the rising and falling of their voices, to the interminable droning, to their sudden silences, and swallowings, more than that, he has been mirroring back, he has been interpreting, but are they appropriate, these words, appropriate to a time when he is both asleep and awake, when it is midday and gray dawn, when this peripheral light is like the return of the repressed, on his chest a huge weight?

Behind the bird, behind the frame on the wall, are the lambent shadows of himself and the other in the room, as if there has been a reversal of light and life, laying bare the transparency, the insubstantiality of the one who has prided himself on helping others. He is being thrust down and out—out where?—where is out?—what is out?—he only knows the thing, the specter on his chest—is it the bird?—is it the woman in the dream?—will not let go—he may even be feeling talons, he is not sure, the fire of its latching to his being is so intense—a waking dream manifest and hidden is being exaggerated to some almost mythic scale, yet all of this is nothing, nothing. . . .

It is the end of the session. Hollister is smiling tearfully. He sees her to the door. She says she is grateful, really greatful, for his help, today has been so helpful. In the tone of her voice, in the seductive thrust of her head there is that coyness of hers, a recurring brittleness that is her weapon against the world. And if that shatters, what will be left to sustain her?

He shuts the door behind her. He stumbles into the bathroom. He swallows an Equanil. He looks in the mirror. The bleariness of his being. Did she, Hollister, see it? No, none of them saw it. They are seeing in him only what they are making of him.

He looks at himself in the mirror, puffed up byond his true being, inflated by his patient's dreams and desires. And then in a sudden shattering of image, he sees himself naked, denuded of all authority.

Thursday night. Twenty-four hours to go and Carol will be home. He returns to the kitchen. The ice clinks. He is drinking again. He sits on the couch. He switches on the Philco. Red Buttons before a live audience. He sees nothing to laugh at. He turns it off. He puts on the record of *The Threepenny Opera*. The sounds are bitter, with aching undertones. "Oh the shark has pretty teeth, dear, and he shows them pearly white. . . ."

He lies on the couch. His heart is pounding, he feels it thudding in his chest, threatening to break out. He gets up and takes another Equanil. He has another drink.

On the table where he placed it when he came in is the evening paper.

News of murders, accidents, storms in the East, advertising, marriages, obituaries, yesterday's news, that is, the news of the things that happened yesterday, that will be replaced tomorrow by today's news. Threats of war but not war—

Inside this house, where at one moment he is the one telling, in the next he is the one listening (with not so evenly suspended attention), here is a memory of the war in the Pacific, of Mercer, the colonel. On Kwajalein he ordered him to take his unit into what he knew, he must have known, would be a suicide mission. He ordered him to do it, and—he did it. He knew even at the time that he should have protested, yet he went, and the men in his unit followed him, and the unit suffered close to one hundred percent casualties, dead, wounded or missing.

What else could he have done? At the time he thought, nothing.

But later in the hospital at home where he recuperated, the man in the next bed, badly wounded in France, told him of a captain in an outfit in North Africa who was ordered to take his men on a suicide mission but refused. "They busted him to lieutenant, then transferred him out, God knows where." "And did the someone else who took over agree to the suicide mission?" he asked. "I don't know," said the wounded man. And then he added, "Probably some general back behind the lines was protecting his own troops, and that was where the order came from."

He tells himself that under such crisis conditions, no one knows ahead of time what he will do. The moment comes, you are under enormous stress, you are never prepared, you have to make a choice. How do you choose? The decision comes, not from thought, not from planning. The decision of a moment.

He has been over it how many times in and out of his own analysis, and now once again, as teller and listener, he tries to extract from it every goddam ounce of guilt and exculpation.

He is suddenly sweating. He opens the glass door to the patio. It is dark and quiet in the garden. This garden has no trees, only low-growing shrubs. Her garden is full of trees.

When they first came to town, he and Jean, the surrounding valley was planted with almond orchards. In the spring, the whole valley bloomed white and pink in the sun. But now the orchards are being uprooted, the land covered over by roads, housing tracts, shopping malls.

And in this garden, it is as if the trees that once stood here have been cut off at the roots, reminding him of *Totem and Taboo*, with its theory of the killing of the father by the sons in the earliest times. . . .

He has not slept, though he has dozed. He has been drinking all night, as well as taking more Equanil, how many he does not know, he has not been counting. With the dawn, he calls the service and tells them to cancel his patients. Only twice before has he done such a thing: when he had to go to the hospital for anxiety (but was it anxiety?—that beating of the heart, that sudden hard beating, they said it was anxiety) and when he had to go back to the Gold Country to get the Jaguar.

When she was his patient, one day she brought in a dream she had as a child, an almost too symbolic dream, as if on order (his order?). She was in the bathtub and a gorilla, hairy and huge, got into the tub with her. At the end of the session, referring back to the dream, he mentioned other dreams and fragments of memories that she'd told him about and suggested a possibility, that her father may have assaulted her when she was a child. She shook her head. He saw that she was not convinced. He too now doubts what he said, wonders why he said it. She seemed to be so sexually repressed. That was the way she presented herself in the office. Later, he was stunned by the passion he found in her. Had she simply deceived him or had she deceived herself? And now she has given him an ultimatum. Saturday. She will be waiting. Let her wait. He will wait her out.

He knew, yes he knew, that the colonel was a fool, good God, he had even spoken with reverence of "The Charge of the Light Brigade." Into the battle, for honor. For honor and death. Yet still, though he knew he was a fool, he obeyed him.

The men trusted him, he had all the marks of authority upon him even then, when he was twenty-eight, and they followed him, seeing in him a depth, a responsibility. They saw reassurance, they saw strength.

He has come to hate that burden.

There's still time to choose a new life. He tells himself he can choose to have another life entirely. Shuffle the cards. Take your pick.

He did it once before.

When he came back from the war, there was, despite what happened with the colonel, the sense of it as a necessary war, a right war. But now that it was over what was he to do? At first, he was uncertain, and then, it was like Fate, when he went back to school he was assigned a professor who directed his reading, and he discovered psychoanalysis. It was a revelation to him, the belief in what is hidden beneath the surface and denied, the belief in the power of the psychoanalyst turning one's own unconscious "like a receptive organ toward the transmitting unconscious of the patient. . . ." The belief that ultimately the irrational can be dealt with rationally— Harry Stack Sullivan even believed it would be possible to avert war through the use of psychoanalytic and psychiatric techniques and research. But Sullivan died already a decade ago in Paris in '49, a suicide, some said. He was found on the floor of his hotel room, pills scattered around him, the medication for his heart condition. He was only in his late forties, early fifties. He had had a schizophrenic episode in his youth, it was suggested.

Was Adams right? Is there some shared thing that is being lived through in all lives now—some break, some shift, some change from what used to be? A change in the power of the superego? That's shit, he thinks. Some shift in the world, in expectation, in allowed expectation—about material things?—not about material things?—in the unconscious—how could that be? In sexuality, as a result of what Freud did, making everything, everyone freer?

Freer? Like hell. Maybe for others, but not for you.

When he was a boy, after his father's death—he died one night working late in the store—his mother had him sleep in her bed. He felt the warmth of her body next to his.

Would he have placed his hands on her, with disgust and excitement feeling his way?

No, he did not.

Someone else did that, a patient, who was it, Armstrong, it was Armstrong years ago, who described sleeping in the same bed as his mother when he was a boy. He said his mother was heavy with huge pendulous breasts, and a big belly. His own mother was small and thin. Shriveled with grief, she lay all night with her thighs tightly closed.

She has given him an ultimatum. Saturday. She will be waiting. Let her wait. He will wait her out.

After he went before the committee of the Institute, he had to wait outside a long time for the judgment. Would they accept him for training or not? He sweated it out. Finally, the door opened. He had stopped sweating by then. Was it that he didn't really care if he was accepted or not? He does not know. He was invited in. He was told he was accepted.

Now if he had to go before a Committee, they would have other questions to ask him, about character, about integrity, about professionalism, about belief. There would be sweating that would not stop.

It is so clear what would happen. He would be called into the room, large and wood-paneled with hanging lights throwing a dim glow over the grave faces of the five who are sitting at a long table, four men and one woman. He would be directed to sit before them in a straight chair. There would be silence while they examine the papers before them.

The woman will begin the questioning. We are interested in that hole in your life, she says.

He sits and thinks, They are trying to trap me.

We are waiting, one of the men says, for your answer.

He decides to report some incidental aspect of his history. He says, When I got out of high school—

Yes?

It was the middle of the Depression so I had to get a job.

And—

By this time we were living in Minnesota. We were living with my mother's family in Minnesota, so I went to work on a farm.

So you worked on a farm?

Yes.

For how long?

For three years.

Did you get paid?

A small amount.

Did you enjoy farmwork?

It was all right.

And what about belief? a white-haired man asks.

So now they have come to the real question. What about belief?

What about your belief?

My mother was religious, my father was not religious.

We're not asking you about your mother or father.

Early on, when I was a kid, I believed, but by this time I had lost my belief.

Those at the table exchange significant glances.

He is full of rage at those significant glances.

He wants to say, What does that have to do with anything?

But he doesn't say it.

He gets up, he announces, I've decided it's not for me.

What is not for you?

All of this.

He is splitting into many, seeing with multiple eyes, their eyes, his own eyes, looking for approval of the great eye, the eyes of the one endowed with God-like qualities in the absence of a god. . . .

Obviously, this is a case of male hysteria, says the white-haired man.

He is remembering—and memory is the preserve of anxiety—he is remembering when he was a resident at the state psychiatric hospital in the days of the back wards, where some patients were kept for years and years, hidden, unseen except by the staff. One woman had been kept there forty years, they were sure she was mad, speaking gibberish, when she was actually speaking a language no one recognized.

And then there was a man, Hodges was his name, he was becoming violent, they tried to stop him, they couldn't stop him by restraining him, so the chief of staff said to give him an injection. If you give me that injection, I'm going to die, Hodges shouted.

They gave him the injection.

He slumped, then he died.

Could one simply say that it was a matter of belief, that he believed so absolutely that he would die if they gave him the injection, that when they gave him the injection he actually died?

Perhaps he should have taken LSD, as Adams suggested. If he would have, there would have been a change, there would have been in his brain, in his sensory apparatus, the equivalent of an eruption, a flaming volcano, seas overflowing, glaciers melting, a great wave coming, forests being uprooted, ground parting in a great earthquake— not this sudden slowing of everything.

Think, think, you are in a room, in your living room, in the house on Creekside Drive you and Carol are renting. There on the table is the newspaper, yesterday's newspaper where you left it when you came in, it is bound with a rubber band. You can just make out a part of a headline—"Eisenhow—" You could go over and take the rubber band off, feel the snap of it against your fingers, you could unfold the paper, you could scan the front page and the pages inside that are filled with words that tell of longing, that tell of loss, that tell of treachery, that tell of betrayal, that tell of suffering—

No, he has not taken his patients' suffering upon himself, like some saint, God knows he is no saint, but there has been a leaking somehow, as if through a porous membrane, from skin through air to skin, a transmission minute but cumulative. That's what it must be. Otherwise, how explain this lassitude, this overwhelming sadness?

What is the key to the lock, that which would make everything fall into place?

The idea of order.

The idea of his disorder, made up of pieces wrested from this one's telling, and that one's telling.

There is no true migration of souls, except in the sense that memories are transferable. In that sense he is left with the memories of others. Leftover debris, his own and others.

He can make no sense of any of this, torn as he is by desire, regret, rage, dissolution.

"I am an angry man," he says to himself. "I am the angry man who believed and disagreed, and believed, and disagreed again. And the more I did not believe, the more tightly I was held by that belief."

He is remembering what Freud said about the uncanny, that it is "the overaccentuation of psychical reality in comparison with physical reality," an infantile element in the minds of neurotics connected to the omnipotence of thought.

Yes, he has overaccentuated psychical reality in comparison with physical reality. Yes, he is being ruled by the omnipotence of thought.

And the howling, she said there was howling, was it so, a dog's howling or his own?

"Oh the shark has pretty teeth, dear. . . ."

Did he bare his teeth, feeling them in his mouth as solid, sharp, hard—for biting, for grasping flesh—but falling out in dreams?

He has just remembered that wooden figure that Lee Adams gave him, which he threw in the back of the Jaguar. He goes out to the driveway. It is dark again. How did it get dark so quickly? He opens the car door. He looks on the floorboard, he can't see it. He searches under the driver's seat and finds it. He shuts the car door. He goes to the side of the house. He drops the wooden figure in the garbage can. He goes back into the house and has another drink.

At this moment he would like nothing better than to be in Vern's life, not to be Vern, but to be in his life, his simple life. Yes, in the woods, yes, hunting when he wants to, yes, when he wants to, mining for gold.

He gets up from the couch and searches for the Gold Country guidebook. It is on a shelf, among the travel books, having been packed and unpacked according to subject by Carol, who is nothing if not orderly. Here is the guidebook, it even has a chapter "Gold Panning for Pleasure," with instructions:

"For an amateur prospector it is advisable to go out to the less accessible streams and creeks which empty into the principal rivers. Look for places where the stream suddenly changes course. Look for sharp turns, look particularly along the inside bend, look for obstacles. You can also work near bedrock, in places that run perpendicular to the stream.

"You will need these supplies: A coffee can, a garden trowel, a small shovel, a handpick, a gold pan, a pry bar, a whisk broom, an old spoon, vials to store the gold dust, tweezers, a magnet, a magnifying glass. . . .

"Facts of interest: The specific gravity of gold is about 19.3 and weighs approximately 1187 pounds per cubic foot. It is the most malleable of all metals. . . ."

As his is the most malleable of lives.

He could fall into any of those lives he hears about every day, but they are not peaceful. This one is peaceful. He is alone. He is living in the woods, he is living in Vern's cabin. In the smoky dimness a strange creature with half a head and five eyes and God knows how many arms is crouching in the corner. Is this pitiful creature the one who called him? The one who made the lunch, almost like a caretaker, something gentle in his caretaking, a kind of gentleness that is not in her, no, not in her, there is a hardness in her.

When I walked away from her house, I turned back and saw the way she looked at me, watching the way I limped.

Does she not have any pity?

Don't tell me pity is what I'm asking for. Has it come down to that? She is right not to give it to me.

Even that is a pitiful statement.

There was always in her—he had sensed it in her even when she was at her most fearful—a wildness that would push everything to the brink. And here he is, almost, he tilts his head backward, gasping for air, on the brink. He could ask for help from one of his colleagues. Why not Craig? He could talk to Craig. He could call him up, but he will not. Shame, yes, of course shame. But it is more than that. There is something about what he is about to go into that he wants to go into, that he needs to go into. A ratcheting up of wish, and risk. The temptation of the brink. . . .

Words of Freud's, read and reread long ago, come back to him with a new emphasis: that the unconscious in its innermost nature is as much unknown as the reality of the external world. As if he is on an edge between the two, the unconscious and the external world, and that is the true locus of his existence.

The landscape is bleak, colorless. A field of wheat lies parched in the hot sun, it has not rained for months. There has been a lapse in his history, a hole in his life, but no longer. In this very moment he is moving through the barrenness of that countryside of his youth, the barrenness he felt about his life as a boy—

After his father's death, his mother moved through the house, silently, doing whatever needed to be done. He sensed she needed him to share her mourning. Soon he became her helpmate in mourning, he became accustomed to its seductiveness.

"'Mourning and Melancholia' is the best thing Freud ever wrote," Schreiber, his training analyst, said.

Schreiber also said, "During the time you are in analysis, you can make no crucial life choices."

So he and Jean had waited four years to get married, four long years. But why do we have to wait? she kept complaining. I have to, he'd said. Why? It's a rule of the analysis. She thought he was a coward to give in to that.

There was a time when he was young when he loved to read Hemingway, admiring in his work all that he wrote about honor, about dignity, about courage in the face of a war-torn world. (Only a step, though a long step, from "The Charge of the Light Brigade" to that.)

He particularly loved *The Sun Also Rises*. Hemingway came out of a different time, a different place. Born before the turn of the century, his childhood summers spent in the upper Michigan peninsula, with its forests, its streams, its fertile greenness, and then going overseas in World War I. . . .

Would he have wanted Hemingway's life?

It is enough for him to say these words to himself, to question his own fate, the fate imposed on him by his own history: An only child, born in New England, North Dakota, on September 10, 1915 . . . etc., etc., etc.

Is this what it is to have a breakdown? To think my words are no good, my thoughts are banal, my body is turning against me with a vengeance and I—I—

I did not expect my life would turn out like this.

Today is Friday. Tomorrow is Saturday. She said, Call by Saturday. Who was she to tell him when to call?

Why did he choose her, and not another, one more pliable, gentler?

Maybe because she was not pliable, not kind, not gentle. There was nothing gentle in her caretaking, that is not in her, no, not in her, there is a hardness in her.

She called it love, but it was never love.

It was simply transference and countertransference.

When he sat with her in the bar of the Gold Rush Hotel, the bartender was polishing a gold Cupid. He was looking at her in the mirror behind the bar. She was telling him a story someone had told her. It was about a man running in a circle in the desert. It might have been the Dakota Badlands.

The landscape is familiar, after all. The car has stopped. The engine has stopped. The fuel pump, the goddammed fuel pump, why didn't he pay attention when he first heard that sound? Now he is going to have to walk a long way, back along the road he has driven with her. He has left her behind, back there where the engine stopped.

He sees a huge rock and beside it a pool of brackish water. A man is lying down and drinking and drinking, his face in the water. He is watching him, he is waiting, he is expecting a nausea, a throwing up, vomiting, and yet more vomiting.

Instead, the man is running. He is running in ever-widening circles. In circles that are stretching to the horizon, so the man is barely visible, and at each turn as he comes around, comes back, he is crying out, I am going to die in this circle, but he does not die, and goes off running into an even wider circle.

Or is there more than one man? Are other men following the running man, they too running in circles, they too crying out in the heat of the sun, the bursting eye of the sun, the gold of the sun?

All the time she is back there, watching him, judging him.

He too can fall into—into perdition. Why that word?

His heart is beating wildly, too wildly.

He must be the running man.

PROBABLY VERN WOULD NOT HAVE LEFT HIS LIFE IN THE GOLD Country, if it had not been for Neal, for Neal's saying what he did. But Neal did come, and after that, Vern no longer wanted to stay where he was.

Neal walked into the cabin that Sunday without advance notice, saying he had gotten a ride up from the city with someone, he didn't say who. Even when he was a kid, when they'd lived in the Midwest, across the street from each other, Neal had been the same way, silent about others' names, like they were things he had to guard, secrets all his own.

Yes, Neal said, he was still living in the city, though he spent four months of the year in Mexico. How he managed to do this without working was a wonder, but then, this was Neal. He had a small pension from having been wounded in the war, and he was frugal. And then too he was always a little loose with rules and other people's property, not criminal exactly, well, maybe a little bit criminal. Yet somehow, when you were with him, he made living on the edge seem not only admirable but enviable.

Maybe it was because wherever Neal was—he'd always felt this, even as a kid—there excitement was. He had a kind of simmering energy, as if he was straining to hold it back, his hooded eyes and his voice suggesting what you'd never think of yourself.

Vern's mother used to caution him that Neal would get him in trouble, that Neal was a bad influence. He'd listen but he wouldn't pay attention. The reason she didn't like Neal, he told himself, was because more than anyone else he knew how to have a good time.

Seeing him again after so long, six or seven years, Vern did notice that he looked a little older, a little thinner, a little balder, and that list of his to the left side when he walked was a little more pronounced. He'd been wounded—in his hip, in his thigh, wherever, Neal never said. What difference did it make, let him have his secrets, Vern was glad to see him.

Since this was Neal's first visit, Vern insisted on giving him the grand tour. He was eager to take him on the back roads, up into the hills, and then into town before coming home. Along the way Neal kept nodding, as Vern pointed out all the good things in this place he had come to call his own.

Late in the afternoon they came back to the cabin and had a beer, sitting outside under the overhang. It was peaceful, it was quiet except for the noise of hundreds of insects buzzing in the high grass. Vern could see how impressed Neal was but then all of a sudden he shifted in his chair and thrust his head forward, as if he was peering into the trees for someone hiding there. "It's so fucking quiet," he said.

"I like it quiet."

"Yeah, quiet like the grave."

"Why do you say that? There's birds and insects and raccoons and deer, and even a fox—"

"Big deal."

"It's country quiet. No traffic. Lots of space. No other house around that I can see." He looked at the trees, at the garden, at the shed, and thought how often, in the evening, just as the sun was setting, he'd sit and think how he had everything he needed right here, nothing was missing.

"What do you do here? There's nothing to do here."

Vern shrugged his shoulders. "Sure there is."

"Like what?"

"A lot of things. I have my work—woodcutting, some carpentry. And I go fishing sometimes, sometimes I go hunting or I go gold panning." And then he added, "I can do just what I feel like doing. Every day I do just what I feel like doing. Nobody tells me—"

Neal laughed his slow-coming laugh. "Jesus, you're just the way you used to be when we were kids. Once you got started doing something, that was it, you'd go down that path and nothing could make you change your mind. If you started playing Monopoly, it was Monopoly ten hours a day, seven days a week, you never got tired of it."

"Neal, what does my liking to play Monopoly when I was a kid have to do with my liking to do what I'm doing now?"

"What I'm saying is"—and here Neal waved his hand in a wide circle—"things are changing out there, the whole universe is changing. Except here, here you sit, you've made a goddam time capsule and sealed yourself into it. You act as if you can keep everything the way it always was."

Trying not to let Neal get to him, Vern said, "I don't see that you've changed so much."

"Oh, I have, I have." Neal was silent for a moment, looking out into the trees, and he pointed his finger right at one of them, as if he was nailing it.

"All I'm saying is," he went on mildly, yet at the same time he seemed to be revving himself up with each word, "how can you call this a life? You call this living, staying in your same hole, doing the same fucking thing today you did yesterday?"

Then he laughed, a little.

Vern got up and went into the kitchen, and brought back two more beers. "Let's just let it go. No point in arguing."

"Who's arguing?" Neal slouched deeper in his chair, his hooded eyes almost closed.

"I'm going to barbecue some ribs for dinner. That all right with you?"

With his eyes shut, Neal nodded. "That's fine with me."

Vern lit some charcoal in the barbecue and then went inside and got the meat and barcecue sauce all ready. When he came out to put the ribs on the fire, wearing his barbecue apron, Neal opened his eyes and surveyed him. "It's great to be waited on by you in your sweet little apron."

"Very funny," Vern said and basted the ribs.

"What do you do for pussy around here?"

"A-ah—" Vern shrugged.

"What's this? You lost interest in that too?"

"No, no. Sometime I—uh—there's a house over in Jackson—"

"Don't tell me you're still paying."

"Yeah, but not all that much, she likes me so she gives me a discount. She's real nice."

"Nice?"

"Yeah, we talk a lot too."

This time Neal's laugh exploded. It went on exploding until he wiped his eyes. "You kill me, Vern. You're still paying when there's free pussy all over the state, all over the country, to say nothing of free talk."

After the dinner, the ribs grilled just right with a smoky tangy sauce, and a big salad with lettuce and tomatoes from Vern's garden, and lots more beer, Neal seemed in a better humor. "Good ribs. Good dinner," he said.

Vern sat there nodding, pleased. The sun was setting. The light was beginning to fade. It was peaceful. Even Neal seemed more peaceful.

"That place called Trail's End—" Neal said. "I remember that story about when you went there."

"No, that wasn't me. It was Ernie Karr."

"I thought you went there."

"No, I never went."

Still, Neal had to go over the story, how soon after the war, Ernie—if that's who it was—kept telling everybody about this really nice place he'd found, way out of town on a side road, a great new place called Trail's End, you could go there and have a drink, it was like a house, just like the living room of a house, with nice furniture, and the people so nice and friendly. So Ernie invited his new girl-friend and her dad to come with him one evening, he thought it would be a good place to take them both and make an impression, and the minute they got in the place, his girlfriend's dad whispered to Ernie, For Christ's sakes, don't you know what this place is? He didn't know it was a whorehouse, he really didn't know. How could you not know? the girlfriend's dad asked him.

Neal looked at Vern and laughed again, his explosive laugh, as if his story really was about Vern after all. It came back to him that along with all the fun you could have with Neal, he could also do this to you, make you feel like a fool.

After a long moment—Neal was staring into the trees again—Vern said, "I don't tell you how to live, do I?"

Neal looked at him. "Don't even try."

"So I don't see why you have to tell me how to live. What difference does it make to you what I do?"

"Let's say I was just being cousinlike, Goosie."

"Don't call me that."

"A term of affection, just like old times."

"I don't like it."

"So I won't call you Goosie. Shit, you can call me anything you want—except late for dinner."

Vern went in the cabin and then he came out again. "What do you want me to do? Give up everything? Just walk out of here and shut the door?"

"What's the big deal? All I'm saying is why not come down to the city and look around? Try it, you might like it."

"I don't know—"

"What do you have to lose? You can always come back to Dullsville."

"But I can't—"

"Sure you can, there's nothing to stop you. Come stay at my pad. I've got a couch. Maybe we'll even go to Mexico."

"Mexico?"

"Why not?"

That night, lying in bed, Vern was seeing with different eyes, even in the dark. It was as though the things in the room that he knew so well, that were almost like part of him, seemed what? less than they had been—duller, flatter. How was it that Neal could have this effect on him? It was as if he was seeing out of Neal's eyes now. But how do you really look with someone else's eyes, don't you have to be in them to do it?

Just yesterday he'd felt so pleased, content with his work, with his garden, with his cabin. He didn't think this place, his life, was dull. Even Edmond, Dr. Edmond, had admired it, and he was surely a man of the world, he knew about places. But then, Vern recollected, Edmond had never called, he had said he would call, but months and months had gone by, and he never did call.

How he hated being called Goosie. In junior high school he wore knickers, his mother made him wear knickers, and his knickers wouldn't stay up on his skinny legs, and maybe because he had red hair and a long skinny neck, and his name was Gosling, they called him Goosie. Who started it, he couldn't remember. The odd thing was that at first he hadn't minded being called Goosie. But when his father heard the other kids call him that, he yelled at him, Why are you letting them call you that? No son of mine should just stand there and let them call you that without knocking their blocks off. He'd had to have a couple of fights, and they'd mostly stopped calling him Goosie.

Neal left the next day, getting a ride from someone—maybe the same someone who brought him, maybe not, he didn't say. From the car he yelled, "Don't forget the invitation. You can crash with me any time."

Would he go, would he not go? Why was he even thinking of going? He went to sleep, saying to himself, I'm not going to go, but then in the morning he woke not knowing if he was or not. He looked out on the garden, he looked into the trees, and it was as if he was slowly starting to disclaim it all.

It reminded him—what the fuck was all this strolling down Memory Lane?—how when he was in high school he was real sweet on this cute girl, Trudy, and finally he got up enough courage to ask her to go out with him, and she said yes, and Neal found out about it, and made so much fun of him in front of the other guys he wrote her a note that said, Don't expect me, I'm not going to go out with you because I'm not—and he finally put down the word "interested." Neal had given him the business and he'd given her the business, so it was somehow even, and he hadn't felt sorry, just relieved.

He didn't question why. You did things. You didn't do other things.

If you needed to know why, you would know why. After all, he wasn't stupid, he could figure a lot of things out by himself, how to fix things, how to make things work, how to cut down a tree, what was the best saw to use, how to track animals, how not to get lost in the woods. . . . Many things came easy to him, natural in a way. What came, came. It was not necessary to act like the world was awash in secrets.

Secrets had something to do with an extra kind of talking, a talking in one's head. As if you had another voice in your head, another person inside your head, whispering words to you. . . . He didn't want that, he didn't believe in that. His life was lived in doing. He ate, he moved, he slept, he worked, he drove, he shat. He felt what he felt—and feeling was rooted in the physical. He felt heat and cold, he felt pain, he felt good in the crisp mountain air, he felt horny, he had felt sad when he had to leave his dog. When things happened, you accepted them. The point was to go on.

If there were moments of darkness, sudden and in the night, when he awakened, wondering, doubting, uneasy at the thought that he was getting older, that he was alone, he said to himself, This happens to everyone once in a while. He stopped himself, it was easy, he had a way of doing that, a simple way. He'd learned it long ago, from his mother. He simply pinched the bridge of his nose between his thumb and his forefinger and it stopped, that wondering that could begin that was like the voice of another, like the voice that kept bugging him to call Dr. Edmond—Edmond— No, he wasn't going to do that. How could he call him when Edmond had said, Don't call me, I'll call you?

CHAPTER

ᜒ 22 ᜓ

THERE WAS TOO MUCH TRAFFIC ON THE BRIDGE, THERE WAS TOO
much traffic everywhere in the city, so it was noon by the time he
got to Neal's, on Eddy Street between Van Ness and Franklin. The
building was old, three stories, an ugly yellow color with the paint
peeling down to the bare board.

The building next door was in the middle of being torn down, but
he saw no workmen around. Most of the outside walls were gone but
there was one interior wall, you could still make out the wallpaper
on it. Across the way was a barbershop with its pole turning and turning, and next to it a motel with neon lights blinking on and off, wast-
ing electricity.

When he got out of the car—he was lucky to find a space right
in front of Neal's building—he was astounded at the noise from the
traffic on Van Ness. He carried the valise up a steep stairway to the

front door, which had no lock on it, so he just walked right in. The entry hall was dark, and had a thick smell, like fish, like cabbage, mixed together. Climbing the stairs, he kept watching that his valise wouldn't bump the wall as the stairway was so narrow. Everything needed painting, the yellow walls, the steps, the banister, the brown apartment doors.

At 3B, on the third floor, he knocked repeatedly but there was no answer, so finally he looked under the mat. The key was there, just as Neal had told him. He unlocked the door and the first thing he noticed when he stepped across the threshold was the dimness, and then the smallness, and then the smell, also like cabbage, also like fish. One small room opened to another small room, with an opening to a little kitchen alcove, and next to it, one step up, the bathroom, its door ajar.

On the double bed, which almost filled the second small room, blankets were thrown every which way, and the sheets, you could see even in the dim light, were filthy. He could hear the din of traffic even in here, coming in through the walls and the two windows facing onto an air shaft. The windows were open and the curtains—also dirty—fluttered in a dusty breeze blowing in the smell of exhaust.

The apartment door opened and Neal came in.

"Oh, it's you," he said.

"You were expecting someone else?"

"No, I wouldn't say that."

"You did invite me," Vern said.

"Sure, I did. I just didn't expect you so soon."

"It's not so soon. It's two weeks." And then he added, "I thought about what you said."

"What did I say?"

"About things changing—"

Vern was taken aback by the look on Neal's face. It was grudging, even sour, when earlier he'd been so insistent. "You did mean that, didn't you?" He was remembering how Neal could sometimes say one thing and mean something else entirely, sometimes even the exact opposite.

"About things changing? Absolutely. I have not changed my mind about that." Suddenly he brightened up. "Well, now that you're here, what do you think of my pad? Not bad for forty bucks a month."

"Nice, it's very nice."

"It's a steal," Neal said. "You should see what they're charging in some places, seventy-five, a hundred for the same thing or even smaller." He walked over to the little table next to the bed and picked up a five-dollar bill that was lying there. "A donation." He grinned. "I lent my pad to a friend this morning, he's got this chick in the office he wanted to fuck, so he asks to use my bed, and I go out, he leaves me five bucks for it, not bad—"

"At least they could have made the bed when they were through."

Neal waved his hand. "It wasn't made when they came." He leaned over the bed and picked up something black, a pair of lace panties. "They must have been in some hurry when they left. She didn't notice she was missing something."

"How could she not notice?"

"I've noticed people don't notice what they don't want to notice." Dropping the panties on the floor, he said, "I'm going to go to the Dented Can. You want to come or you want to stay here?"

"I'll come," Vern said. "What's the Dented Can?"

"An experience," Neal said.

The Dented Can was in a warehouse in the Mission. Lights on long cords hung from a high ceiling. Open boxes with cans—some with

big dents, some with little dents—were stacked in rows. Canned veg-
etables, canned fruit, canned tuna, canned meat, the stacked cans went
on and on, though not in any particular order. Everything was at
least half off the regular price you'd pay in a grocery store. The cans
with big dents were even less than that.

Much to Vern's surprise, Neal was a cautious shopper. He looked at
every single can, turning it round and round and upside down. "In
case it's punctured, you don't want it. You could get botulism from it."

"You looking for anything special?"

"With big dents, but not punctures."

After getting some cans of corn and green beans and peas and
tomatoes and tuna, Neal said, "Now comes the good part." He led Vern
to a section of cans without labels. "These, they practically give away."

"What are they?"

"No one knows. It's like a lottery. By now I know enough to
know that those small ones are food, mostly beans. I got enough
beans, I don't need beans. But these, these others," he picked up one
of the large cans, "my guess is, this is paint."

"What do you want it for?"

"What do I want it for?" He paused. "It just came to me, I could
paint a wall."

"But you don't know the color."

"Whatever color comes out of the can, that's the color I'll paint
the wall."

When they got home, Neal opened the paint, and it turned out to
be a fiery red. "I should paint that wall," he pointed to the wall
behind the bed. "That could liven up bedtime."

"I guess," Vern said.

A phone was ringing in the hallway, and after a minute there was
a knock on the door.

"Telephone, Neal," someone called out.

Shortly he was back. "I have to see a man about a dog."

"What dog?"

"For Christ's sakes, it's a manner of speaking, Goosie."

Vern said, "Don't—" and Neal held up his hand. "I won't say it again, it slipped out."

Vern would have liked to ask Neal how long he would be, but he knew a straight question never got a straight answer from him, so he decided not to.

Vern hadn't eaten since morning, so he looked in the refrigerator. All he found was a six-pack and some moldy cheese. He thought about opening one of the dented cans of corn, but he couldn't find a can opener in any of the drawers in the kitchen alcove. He sat down on the couch, which had had one of those Army blankets from the Army surplus store over it to cover the holes underneath, only since the blanket also had holes in it, some of the couch holes were still showing.

He had an urgent impulse to clean up Neal's pad. He could see what needed to be done, the sheets needed to be taken to the Laundromat, if there was a Laundromat near by, there must be, the floor had to be washed and maybe even polished, the bathroom, it was a mess, it really needed Clorox and then more Clorox, the tub was grimy, almost black—but he restrained himself. This wasn't his place, and besides maybe Neal wanted it just like this, cluttered, okay, dirty.

He sat for a while, feeling aimless, hanging between something and something, perhaps between some place and no place. He turned his head, and looked at the bed, at the table, at the kitchen alcove. He saw the open can of paint on the kitchen counter. It occurred to him that he had an old drop cloth in the backseat of the car, he had an old paintbrush, he had rags. He didn't have any paint thinner, though. He went over to the paint. He could tell by the smell that it was a water-based paint. He didn't need paint thinner.

A couple of hours later, he had half of the wall painted. He couldn't do any more because he'd run out of paint. After he washed the brush in the kitchen sink, he went downstairs and replaced the brush and the drop cloth in the pile of things on the backseat. He'd been right not to throw those things out. You could never tell what emergency might come up tomorrow, and you'd need something desperately, only to realize you'd thrown it away yesterday.

Back in the flat, he turned on the one lamp, sat on the couch and studied the wall. The unpainted and the painted parts lay next to each other, not blending, uneasy side by side. First he looked at the red. Then he looked at the tan. After he'd been looking at the red, the tan looked old and grayish, worse than before. And when he looked at the red after looking at the tan, it seemed garish, too shiny, and moreover there were places where, he now saw, the red didn't cover and the tan was showing through. He should probably go back to the Dented Can and get another can of paint just like this one, but how would he know what color paint he was getting, since there were no labels on any of the cans? And for all he knew he could get a can that might not even be paint.

He should have left well enough alone.

Forget it, he told himself, it's a wall, nothing but a goddam wall. Still, there was something weird about it. Looking at it made him feel weird, like he was looking at a map of his life, laid out before him. He had lived one life, and then he had covered over—wiped out— that life with another life, an entirely different life, or he thought he had, but the old one managed to leak through when you were least expecting it—

The door opened and Neal came in puffing after climbing the two flights. His head was bald.

"What the fuck happened here?"

"I painted the wall."

"Half a wall—"

"I ran out of paint."

Neal frowned and was silent for a moment. "You know what? I like it. It's got character. It adds a special touch." He rubbed his hand over his scalp.

"What happened to you?" Vern asked.

"You mean the no-hair. I went by the barber college. They had a sign. Student haircut, seventy-five cents. I went in and said, Shave it. This creep says, 'We're not doing shaves today.' I said, 'The hair, the hair, shave the hair.' How do you like it?"

"It's clean."

"And cheap. Don't forget cheap."

They each had a beer, and some corn from a can—it turned out the can opener was in the bathroom cabinet—and some tuna fish from a can. Afterward, Neal sat on the couch and looked at the wall. "I really like that wall," he said. "The longer you look, the more things you see in it. Like there"—he pointed—"do you see, it looks like a face, a face with horns on the top?"

"I don't see it," Vern said.

It was after eleven that night when they started out for some party Neal had been invited to. They walked in the fog through darkened streets, the fog making everything softer, the street lights softer, even the sounds of cars softer. Vern was just following Neal, not paying attention to what street came after what street, to where they turned. At last they came to a busy intersection with lots of lights, with streets coming off of it with all sorts of shops with junk for tourists, and then they came to an even busier section with crowds of people on the street talking and laughing, some going into places and some coming out, places like nightclubs with neon signs and strip joints, with pictures with women with huge tits displayed out front.

They came to a corner building—that is, it was on a angled corner, and the building itself ended in a sharp angle. Inside, upstairs, people were milling about, everybody was helping themselves to liquor, lots of loud music, very loud, lots of smoke. Neal pushed him forward, and said, "Folks, meet my country cousin." People looked at him, he felt shy for a moment, but then no one paid him any attention. He got himself a drink and then another. He was sitting alone. He was feeling he didn't belong. He was thinking maybe he should go back to the pad. Neal came over and handed him a lumpy cigarette. Vern said, "I don't smoke." Neal said, "Try this, you'll like it."

He tried it. It didn't do much for him. Someone gave him another one. After a while he noticed he wasn't feeling lonely. He was coming to feel maybe this was where he should be, with all these nice people. He looked over at Neal, who at the moment had an arm around one blonde woman, while another blonde hung close to him on the other side, rubbing his head with her hand. Everyone in the room was talking and laughing so easily, riding along on a wave of some kind, skimming along, never getting stuck, just gliding by.

Shortly he found himself talking first with this one, then with that one, saying whatever was coming into his head—everyone was laughing—he was laughing—his thoughts connected to their thoughts, not like the talking he had done before.

If you'd asked him yesterday when he'd finished the job on the pine if he was going to be here, doing this, he would have said, You're out of your mind. But here he was.

No matter what he'd thought, no matter what he'd said to that girl, what was her name, the one with Edmond, about not wanting change, he must have wanted it, to come here.

He had this sudden sense—he wondered if others had it—you go along one way, and then without your expecting it your life changes, you change.

Where is the old you? Hiding? Hiding where? Left behind in his cabin, more than miles, like centuries away. Or was he both at the same time? It was hard to tell here in this corner apartment that was itself a corner, with so many odd angles.

Did I forget to lock the shed? he asked himself.

No, he'd locked it. He remembered locking it before he left and then he shut the cabin door behind him. It was a good thing he hadn't gotten a dog yet. He wouldn't have liked leaving the dog alone.

CHAPTER

c~ 23 ~ɔ

WHEN VERN WOKE UP IN THE MORNING, HIS BACK WAS ALL awry from having slept on the couch. Its broken springs had jutted into him, no matter which way he'd turned. His head was clogged, his mouth was dry. He smelled a strong smell—of fish, of cabbage, of paint. He sat up and shook his head slowly. He looked at the wall. In the gray morning light it was just a wall, half painted.

Neal hadn't come home yet.

As he couldn't find any coffee in the kitchen, just an empty jar of instant, he went across the street to the motel coffee shop. He ordered coffee, he wasn't up to food. The noise of plates banging, of people talking, hurt his ears.

On his way back across the street, he checked on his Buick. He had parked it in the driveway of the house that was being torn down next door. Neal had told him to park there so he wouldn't get a ticket.

No, he said, they wouldn't be working there today. They hadn't worked there for months.

When he got upstairs, he took a shower in the grimy tub and dried himself with a grimy towel. Then he shaved. In the mirror his eyes were bloodshot, his skin was blotched with patches of red. He looked hungover, bleary. Little black dots kept appearing in front of his eyes. They were like tiny flies or specks of dust that vanished as soon as he tried to focus on them. He was seized by the crazy idea, it sure was crazy, that his cabin had also vanished, as if it was a person he had walked out on, and he was going to be punished for leaving it.

He started cleaning up the place. He stripped the sheets off the bed, he collected the few towels, he went out to a Laundromat, which he found on the next block, where they would wash, dry and fold things for you. In a small mom-and-pop shop around the corner he bought some cleaning supplies. Just thinking about how he was going to get rid of the dirt and grime made him feel better.

He'd cleaned the bathroom and the kitchen, and had just finished washing the floors when Neal came in. "What happened to you, last night?" he asked.

"I could ask you the same thing," Vern said.

"Last I saw of you, you looked like you were having a ball dancing—"

"I was dancing?"

"You don't remember?"

"No, I don't—but—wait a minute—there was some music—I remember that—the same melody over and over again, only getting louder each time it was played—yeah, and I was—"

"Like a whirling dervish. But the next time I looked you were gone. You didn't tell me you were leaving."

"I guess I didn't see you."

"I was in the bedroom with the girls." Neal grinned. "So—I've got a great day planned for us."

"I'm not up to any more partying."

"Who said anything about partying? We're going to Big Sur."

"What's in Big Sur?"

"You'll find out. We'll take your car."

"I have to stop at the Laundromat first, to pick up the sheets and towels."

"Leave it to later. I want to get on the road. We've got to make a stop on the way, in Sunnyvale."

He hadn't said a word about the cleaning. Maybe, he just didn't notice.

On the way Neal explained—it was not like him to explain, but last night must have put him in an explaining mood—that he had to stop to see Lila. She'd called last week and asked him to come by. She'd just arrived from Mexico and was staying in Sunnyvale with her mother, and she had a Mexican wedding shirt she wanted him to give to George, whoever George was.

It'll only take a minute, he said, when they parked across the street from Lila's mother's house. It had a front yard filled with rocks and small, spiky plants, in imitation of a desert. Vern watched as Neal walked up the cement path, swaggering a little more than usual. He knocked on the door and a woman with big blonde hair opened it. When she saw Neal, she screamed, "Your hair! What did you do to your hair?"

Vern didn't hear what Neal said, but he saw Neal bow his head and Lila, it must be Lila, put out her hand and rub his scalp. Then Neal and Lila had a conversation, which ended with Neal waving to Vern, and yelling to him to come in, Lila had invited them to have something to eat. So here Vern was sitting on the couch in Lila's mother's living room, while Neal and Lila were out in the kitchen, with the swinging door closed.

Lila's mother was sitting ramrod straight in her big chair, her legs thick and swollen. She was so still and unforgiving-looking, she seemed like a figure made of stone. Vern tried to start a conversation with her out of politeness, it was her house, after all, and she was an older lady, but she didn't answer. He didn't think she was deaf, she couldn't be deaf, she was watching TV, and at the same time she must have been listening to what was going on in the kitchen. Though the door was closed, there were a lot of thumping and bumping noises coming through it, and at one point she called out, "What are you doing, Lila?"

"Nothing, Ma." It was a muffled voice.

Lila's mother seemed to be satisfied with that, at least she kept on watching the TV show, a man and a woman were having an argument, he couldn't follow why, but then he never watched television. He didn't even have a TV.

The noises from the kitchen suddenly got louder. "What are you doing, Lila?" Lila's mother called out again. And after a moment came the same reply, "Nothing."

What did she think Lila was doing? Or was she asking not to know, to get the answer, Nothing?

He yawned. The day was warm and the heat had invaded the house. He was thinking of his own cabin among the trees—yes, it was still there, of course it was still there—even when it was hot, there was a special quality to the heat. You could almost smell the earth, the odor of pines, whereas here the smell was of plaster walls and plastic upholstery.

The screen door banged and a kid in overalls came in, about ten or eleven, with thick dark hair and very dark eyes, and he sat down on the couch next to Vern and started watching television without saying a word.

Soon after, Lila opened the swinging kitchen door and came in, her big hair a little disheveled, carrying mats and napkins and silver. Behind her was Neal, carrying some plates. His bald head was shining.

"Don't set a place for me," Lila's mother said, her eyes not turning away from the screen.

"You have to have something."

"I'm not hungry. I'll eat later."

"You go and wash your hands, Pedro," Lila said. The boy didn't move, he just sat there watching.

"Pedro, did you hear me tell you to wash your hands? Go wash your hands, or I'm going to turn off the TV."

"Don't turn off the TV," said Lila's mother.

Pedro got up and began backing out of the room, his eyes on the screen.

"This is Neal. That's Vern," Lila said. "You know how to say hello." But the boy drifted out without a word.

Lila sighed. "It's not easy to get his attention. You have to scream sometime to get him to listen."

"That's the trouble with kids, these days," said Neal. "They don't pay attention. And I'll tell you why. It's because they haven't been trained to pay attention, their parents don't train them."

"Children are not dogs," Lila's mother said.

"He's only talking, Ma. He doesn't know anything about kids."

"Don't I? Anybody can see, you don't have to be an expert to see the kid needs discipline, and he's not getting it. He's like all the other kids now, all they know is me—me—me—I want—I want—I want—"

"Look who's talking," said Lila.

"What are you saying? You think I think only of me-me-me? Not true. Just not true. You must be thinking of somebody else. This is Neal"—he tapped himself on the chest—"the cat with a bent frame, the one who's into helping others, who always wants to do good unto others. Ask Vern. He'll tell you."

"What is the man talking about?" said Lila's mother. "What cat?"

"He—he was wounded in the war."

"In the war?" Lila's mother said, staring at Neal.

"Yes, ma'am, I was wounded in the war."

"Where?" asked the kid, who had just come back into the room.

"Where, what place, or where, which part of my body?"

The boy shrugged.

Neal moved close to the boy and looked down at him. "You really want to know?"

The boy nodded warily.

"Usually I don't talk about it, but this time, since it's you asking, this time I will." Neal stood silently for a moment, hands at his side. "I was in the Pacific—

"Are you listening?"

The boy nodded, and the next thing, much to Vern's surprise, Neal was telling about his squad being sent out on patrol, they weren't expecting enemy fire, they were crossing a clearing in the jungle, when suddenly out of nowhere the shooting started, the Japs were shooting at them, the sergeant was yelling "Move! Take cover!" and he was running like hell but just before he got to the line of trees he tripped and fell into a kind of a gully, he could hear the sergeant yelling, "Move! Move!" he could hear the bursts of fire, but how was he going to move when he couldn't even stand up? He'd been hit, he hadn't even known he was hit.

"What did you do?" the kid asked, staring at Neal as if he couldn't tear his eyes away.

Vern too was staring at Neal because instead of telling it like it was some joke, which Vern was expecting, he was telling it seriously. At least, his face was serious. His eyes were wide open. His voice was deeper, slower. Vern was used to being an audience for Neal, he always had been, but this time it was different, there was something different in Neal's face, as if, as he was talking, he was listening to himself, as if he was part of his own audience—that's what it seemed like to Vern.

"Do? There wasn't much I could do. They were still firing. My squad had run off and the Japs were after them. There I was, lying there, my heart beating so hard I was sure they'd hear it. They were running right by me, no more than a few feet away from me, I couldn't believe they didn't see me. Then—after a while, they were gone but I knew there would be more of them coming any time."

"Did they come?"

"Yeah, they came. They passed me right by too. I couldn't believe it. I tried to cover myself with leaves and twigs but I couldn't even do that. All I could do was just lie there."

"How long?"

"Times like that you don't know how long. Two, three days and nights . . . it's raining . . . and the insects . . . and I'm lying there in the mud and my own blood and piss and shit—"

Lila's mother gasped. It could have been in pity, it could have been in doubt, or maybe she just wasn't used to that kind of language.

"In my own blood and piss and shit," Neal repeated. "I kept wanting to crawl somewhere but I couldn't move, so I made myself be still, I said to myself, It's up to you to look still as the dead."

"How do you do that?" the boy asked. "How do you stop your breathing?"

"I don't know what the doctors would say, but I told myself I could do that."

"Then what happened? How did you escape?"

"I didn't escape, I stayed there. But then, at some point, I don't know when it changed, things changed, and one of our squads, not my squad, another squad, came by on patrol, and they—they found me there, and they carried me back to the line. There I found out that my squad, the ones that ran off and left me, they were all killed. I was the only one to survive."

"That's a terrible story," Lila's mother said.

"Yes, ma'am, it is a terrible story. You kind of lose your faith in other people, that they'd run off like that and leave you—"

"Maybe they thought you were dead."

"They knew I wasn't dead."

"Maybe they were going to come back for you later."

"Maybe, but we'll never know, will we?"

"What choice did they have? If they thought they would be killed if they stayed, what choice did they have?"

"You're right, ma'am. What choice did they have? I can say that now, but then—"

In the silence a commercial was blasting, real loud, advertising Lux soap.

"It was all a long time ago," Lila said impatiently.

"Not so long," said her mother.

"How long?" said the kid.

"Long before you were born," Lila said.

"Are you a religious man?" Lila's mother asked Neal.

"No, I wouldn't say I was a religious man. Why do you ask?"

"You must feel that someone was watching over you—when you think about it—"

"I try not to think about it but sometimes I do think about it, when I least expect it. Say, I'm at a party, celebrating, having a good time, then all at once I start to think that the ones who left me to die, died, and I survived, and you think, This is telling me something: I am here because they left me to die."

They waited for Neal to say more but he didn't go on.

Lila gasped, "The beans! I forgot all about the beans." She rushed out into the kitchen, but in a minute she was back. "I had them on a low flame, thank God, so nothing burned."

Neal turned to Vern. "It's late. I didn't realize how late. We got to be on the road, man."

"What do you mean, you're not going to have anything?" she wailed. She turned to Vern. "Aren't you hungry, Vern?"

"Well," he said.

"We'll pick something up on the way," Neal said.

"That's crazy," Lila said, "Everything's all ready. It'll just take a few minutes."

"When you gotta go, you gotta go," Neal said, and started out the door.

"Wait, wait a minute, the shirt, you have to take the shirt for George. I'll get it. Just a minute."

"Oh yeah, the shirt for George, that's right."

"And I've got some papers I wanted you to look at—"

When Neal and Vern got outside, they had to walk around a car parked in front of the house to cross the street. In an instant, Neal had opened the rear door, and pulled out a leather jacket lying on the seat.

"What are you doing?" Vern asked.

"The jacket was there waiting, just asking to be taken. Who could say no?"

Vern laughed, despite himself. "How do you know it'll fit you?"

"It'll fit well enough, I can tell. Now I've got a nice wedding shirt and a leather jacket to go with it," and he threw them both on top of the pile of things in the backseat of the Buick, along with an envelope Lila had given him.

As they pulled away, he looked at the other houses on the street. "I can't believe Lila's living in a house like that— Did you see all those goddam figurines? Shepherds and shepherdesses—"

"I didn't notice."

"—living in the middle of all that crap on a street with every house like every other house."

"It's her mother's house."

"So what's the difference if it's her mother's house, she's living in it."

"I don't know. It doesn't seem so terrible to me. If you look around, it's a nice little neighborhood, with lots of trees."

"You would think so," Neal said.

After they'd been driving a while, Vern said, "What you said back there—"

"What about it?"

"I just wondered—was it—was it the true story?"

"You want to know if it was true?"

"Yeah."

"True enough." He looked out of the side window. "Jesus, there must be hundreds more of these same houses going on for miles."

"People need places to live."

Neal turned and looked at Vern, his eyelids low once again. "The way I look at it, it's a good thing to shake people up, get them out of their old ways of thinking, you know, break things up a little. You stir up this, you stir up that, so it's a whole new ball game—you stir up the pot—sorry, I mean the container—these days, I don't even say 'Pot-rero Hill,' I say 'Containerero Hill.' You never know who might be listening."

"Who might be listening? There's nobody here but us."

"You're right, Vern, you're absolutely right. Any other questions?"

"Where's the kid's father?"

"The question is who is the kid's father—Lila herself doesn't know with all the screwing around she was doing at that time, fucking anything that moved or maybe that didn't even move." Then Neal added, "It's a wise father who knows his own child."

"I don't get it," Vern said, but Neal was already asleep, his head having fallen to one side.

As they were driving down the coast through Seaside, all of a sudden, Neal woke up. He said he was starving, he couldn't go another minute without a burger. They stopped in front of a small café. The air was cool, fog was coming in from the ocean, so Neal put on the leather jacket. "I told you it was meant for me. Fits me to a tee."

They each ordered a burger and fries and a beer, and while they were waiting, Neal opened the envelope Lila had given him, and unfolded the two pages that were inside. He'd just been reading a minute or so when he burst out laughing so loud the other people in the café turned to look at him. "Listen to this," he tried to calm himself, but then he started laughing again until tears came to his eyes. "You gotta hear this, you won't believe this," he gasped.

"What is it?"

"This is Lila's idea for a vacation resort. Or rather Lila's idea as George wrote it up for her, and that's why she bought him a wedding shirt."

"Lila owns a resort?"

"She doesn't own it exactly, she's put some money in it, and she's sure she's going to make a killing. She's out of her mind. Just listen to this: 'At the Villa of Peace'—that's what she calls it—'you will find palm-thatched huts under coconut trees, an immense jacaranda tree spreading its benevolent branches, wild orchids, papayas, beautiful sights, wonderful smells, all making for a unique shelter and escape from the stresses of modern life. This tropical paradise is indeed Tahiti, Moorea and Bora-Bora all rolled into one.' Lila, the great expert on Tahiti and Moorea and Bora-Bora—"

The waitress brought their burgers and fries, and Neal put the papers down. But after a while, he picked them up and started to read again in a singsong voice. "'Everywhere one looks is a feast for the eyes. The people are gentle and kind. Never is heard a harsh word. Here one lives an outdoor, barefoot existence without discomfort. The atmosphere is unorganized and uncontrived. It is a place to enjoy nature and to read, to talk and to contemplate.'" On the last word he fell into a spasm of coughing.

"Take it easy, you'll choke."

After he caught his breath, Neal said, "You have to know Lila to really appreciate this. Her idea of contemplating is on her back, with her legs spread.

"There's more. 'One look at this paradise will convince you. We have at our disposal clean, well-appointed palapas (native style huts) that you can rent by the day for 62.50 pesos (five dollars!!) including all meals. We are preparing now for our season and reservations are coming in fast. . . .'

"Five bucks for a grass hut and a privy," Neal said. "I guarantee you, it'll never fly."

"Oh, I don't know," Vern said. "It sounds like a pretty good deal to me."

"It would," Neal said in disgust, throwing the papers on the table. "Come on, let's go, it's getting dark, and that Highway One is a bitch at night."

Vern followed him out of the café, but before leaving, he picked up the papers about the Mexican paradise and put them in the back pocket of his jeans. Someday, he just might go there.

CHAPTER

ᑎ 24 ᕷ

GOING SOUTH ON HIGHWAY I, VERN DROVE SLOWLY. AS HE
followed one curve after the other, the fog kept shifting. In some
places the road was clear, the shoulder visible. In other places, the fog
was like a wall, throwing the glare of the headlights back at him.
At times he could make out the lights of another car coming in the
opposite direction, just before it came to the curve, and he edged
over as far as possible. To his left the road was built into a cliff, and to
his right everything dropped away steeply. In the dark he couldn't see
how steeply but an image came to him of a car hurtling over the side
and falling into the sea. He was surprised at his own imagining.

Hearing Neal snore, he glanced over at him. His head had fallen
forward, and in the light from the dashboard, his face looked slack,
the skin hanging. The leather jacket he had ripped off from the car
had hunched up around his neck. It didn't fit him right, after all.

Suddenly Vern felt pity for Neal, but Neal wouldn't want, didn't need pity. And besides, people, when they slept, always looked different from when they were awake, they couldn't defend themselves against prying eyes.

He followed the coast road for thirty miles or so until it turned inland. Soon the fog had thinned to a mist. On both sides of the road tall trees rose up, redwoods and pines, he could tell, even in the dark. From the way they were clustered, they were probably second growth. He felt reassured, even so, by the way they seemed to be standing guard.

At last he saw the turnoff Neal had told him to look out for. He almost missed it, he had to brake hard. He turned right onto a dirt road, following it down to a flat open area, where he parked in front of a brightly lit one-story building. Scattered nearby were other smaller structures, dark except for an outside light burning at each door.

He must have been clutching the wheel, the way his neck and shoulders had tightened up. He got out of the car, and shook his head back and forth and up and down and in a circle, and lifted his shoulders up and down, and waved his arms around until he felt things loosen up. All the time he kept sniffing this smell, part ocean, part trees, part mist, part dampness from the ground, not like the Gold Country, not peaceful, more complicated than peaceful, exciting in the way a scent can be exciting.

"We're here." His voice was loud in the silence—but Neal didn't wake up. He went around to the passenger side and opened the door and shook him lightly, then shook him again.

"What? What?" Neal said, his eyes staring, but looking around as if he couldn't see anything.

"It's okay, it's okay, it's me, Vern."

"What—? Where—?"

"We're in Big Sur, we just got here—we drove down—"

It was like a light had been switched on in Neal's eyes. "Yeah, yeah, I know, you don't need to tell me." He looked down at the leather jacket. "Nice jacket." He pummeled his chest with both fists, in a clownish imitation of King Kong. "So, now we're here, what are we waiting for?" He was back to the old Neal, his voice back to its old suggesting, I know how to have a good time, just follow me.

He got out of the car and pulled the jacket down so it didn't hunch up around his neck. "I need to pee bad," he said, and moved off to the side of the building.

The fog here was not thick, but moving, drifting, and you could hear the sound of waves crashing out beyond the buildings where the cliff must end. Vern thought he heard a bird cry, maybe a gull, but he didn't know if gulls cried at night.

When Neal came back, Vern said, "You're sure this isn't a private place?"

"It's not private, believe me."

"But how do you know?"

"Someone told me."

"You mean you haven't been here before?"

"No, but someone told me."

Vern knew better than to ask who "someone" was.

Inside, the lit-up building was, no doubt, a public place. There was a regular bar to sit at and a mirror behind the bar, with liquor bottles stacked on shelves. Off to the side of the bar was an open area with a few tables, and beyond that space was a closed double door. The place was empty except for the bartender, a young guy with bushy hair. Neal and Vern sat at the bar, and each ordered a beer.

"Where is everybody?" Neal asked.

The bartender pointed to the double door. "They're still in the seminar."

"What kind of seminar would that be?"

"It's on mind-body."

"What's mind-body?" Vern asked Neal.

"You got a mind. You got a body. What more do you need to know?"

After some time, they were still the only ones drinking, and Neal got restless. He kept glancing at the clock on the wall behind the bar as if he had an appointment and was afraid he'd be late. From beyond the double doors came different muffled sounds, a scream, loud voices calling out, laughter, and then something like a long drawn-out sigh. Finally, after a long silence, the double doors opened and a man came out, and then a woman, and soon they were followed by others, men and women, mostly young, though a few older. Some were talking, some were silent, one woman was wiping her eyes. With the doors open, you could see into a big room with chairs around the edges, and pillows at the center.

Several people came over and sat at the bar. One man sat on the other side of Neal, and Vern heard Neal ask him about the screaming, and the man said, It was nothing, it was just part of the seminar, but then he clammed up, he didn't seem to want to say anymore.

A young woman came and sat next to Vern. She was pretty, slim and dark, wearing glasses. The bartender asked her what did she want. She looked down at her nails, which were bitten to the quick. "Could I have a Coke, please?"

Her hand shaking, she took out a cigarette. Vern offered her a light from the book of matches lying on the counter. "Thanks," she said. Her smile was hesitant. Her Coke came and she stubbed out her cigarette, but she sat there without picking up her drink, and then she took out another cigarette.

"Are you okay?" Vern asked, as he offered her a light for the second cigarette.

"I'm fine, I'm just—shaken up," and she mumbled something about going through a lot "in there." Behind the glasses, her eyes were a soft, almost liquid brown.

"Like what?"

"So much happened, it's hard to talk about." But then, a moment later, she was talking. Out came a rush of words, something about an inner journey, and then she bit her lip and the words slowed down, and then another rush of words, ". . . where you've never been, where you've always wanted to be. . . ."

Neal poked Vern in the ribs, and in a low voice said, "How are you making out?"

"I'm just talking to her, that's all I'm doing."

Vern turned back to the girl. She was drinking her Coke now. He noticed the smoothness and whiteness of her throat, as she tilted her head back. "Do you know all those people who were in there with you?" he asked her.

"Are you kidding, I never met them before. That's the whole point, that you're strangers to each other." She was getting more and more excited as she talked about how you start out with a group of people you don't know at all and after a while they start to talk and soon they're talking about things they would never tell to people even if they really know them well, and soon everybody is so involved, it's like one person's secret leads to everybody's secret . . .

"It's called spilling your guts," Neal said sourly in Vern's ear, but Vern ignored him.

"I never thought I could do that, say personal things in front of a whole group of strangers. At first I wondered why I even came but soon, I don't know how it happened, I was talking about myself—" She took a swig of the Coke and swallowed hard.

"It's amazing," she ducked her head shyly, "when you start saying things that you've never said to anybody, you come to realize how you've been putting on a show so as not to let anybody know who you are. But in there, with all those people listening, you can't get away with that. Once you start talking, once you allow yourself to really be in there, you give up all that pretending and you begin to find out who you really are."

"Do you really want to know?" Neal said loudly, leaning across Vern.

Vern was embarrassed, because he was worried she would get upset, but in fact, she said, "I wouldn't have come here if I didn't want to know."

"Hey, do you have a pay phone around here?" Neal asked the bartender.

"Outside, turn left," the bartender said.

Neal slid off the bar stool, put his hand inside his jacket and in a mock heroic pose, said to Vern, "I shall return."

"Your friend is certainly, well, antagonistic," the young woman said. "Why does he come here, if he feels that way?"

"He didn't come here for a seminar. We were just passing through and stopped off."

"Still, he ought to know that other people come here with a serious purpose in mind and he shouldn't—"

"He didn't mean anything by it. It's just his way of talking." He asked her if she wanted another Coke. "Maybe I'll have a martini," she said.

"I'll join you," he said, though he never drank martinis.

While they sat there drinking and talking, he kept looking at her. There was something sweet about her, sweet and maybe a little bit sad and innocent somehow, even her excitement was innocent. She was so caught up in what she'd just been through in the seminar, she didn't ask him anything about himself, what work he did, where he came from. Somehow that made him feel free and easy, even freer and easier than at the party, what he remembered of it. You were here, you'd arrived here, and you were starting from scratch. It could go any which way.

He asked her about the body part of a "mind-body" seminar. "Do you do exercises or something?"

"Not exactly exercises, though maybe you could call them that. You know, there are lots of different seminars and each seminar leader has his own thing. But in ours, what we did, at one point the leader had us all came close together and one person at a time, they throw you up in the air, and they catch you in a blanket—"

"And what does that do?"

"Well—uh—it's supposed to—you're supposed to learn to trust the other people, not be afraid that they will drop you."

Neal, who had returned to his seat at the bar, leaned across Vern and said, "So when you get all this terrific trust going, then what?"

She flushed. "It's not a joke."

"I didn't say it was. I just want to know. Then what?" Neal asked in his most innocent tone, which was not really very innocent.

"Then, well—" She hesitated but then she went on boldly, as if the words themselves were special words, freeing words. "You come to realize your old fears are not real fears but they are false fears. All the things you've stopped yourself from doing all your life because other people said not to, and because you yourself internalized their prohibitions—you're not going to be stopped anymore. You finally are going to be able to choose what you really want, you learn what you really want."

"Sounds good to me," Vern said.

The girl smiled gratefully at him.

"So can you say what you really want?" Neal asked, his eyes hooded more than ever.

"You mean me? What I want?"

Neal nodded.

"Not yet, but I hope I'll find out."

"Lots of luck," Neal said. And then he added, "So what if somebody wants something that somebody else doesn't want?"

"What do you mean?"

"Say somebody takes a dislike to somebody else and what he wants more than anything else is to beat the shit out of them."

"No, no, that doesn't happen. They wouldn't allow that. The negative feelings come out, of course they have to come out, they tell you that at the beginning. You're allowed to say them but you're not allowed to do them. It isn't—you know—like anarchy. That's why they have a leader. You have to feel safe. Otherwise you wouldn't let yourself say what you have to say. You wouldn't let yourself take the risk. They tell you at the beginning that it's no easy thing to be stripped of your defenses, to open yourself up, to open yourself—to—" and she frowned, as if she had to be sure to choose the right word, "to the universe."

"That is one fucking big opening," Neal said. "Well," he patted Vern on the back, "I have to go try my call again. You want to step outside with me for a moment?"

"I'll be right back," Vern said to the girl.

At the black phone booth Neal dialed, then after a moment, he hung up. "The line's still busy." He kicked at the ground with his boot. "This place is driving me nuts."

"So why did we come? You were the one who wanted to come here."

"Someone told me they had a terrific time here, picked up a couple of girls—but not like her, not like that girl. 'You'll come to realize your old fears are not real fears but false fears,'" he added in a falsetto.

"She was just saying what happened in the seminar."

"You know how much people pay to be in one of these seminars? Hundreds of bucks, someone told me, hundreds of bucks. Whoever runs this place, I can tell you, is con artist of the year. All this talk, talk, talk, and all the time it is only one more mind fucking system."

"But—" Vern said.

Neal held up his hand and went to the phone and dialed again. This time he got an answer, and he kept nodding his head and saying, Yeah, yeah. Finally, he hung up. "He told me how to get there, it's just a couple of miles down the road."

"Who's he?"

"He is some cat who lives near here who has lots of anything you'd want."

"I'll take you over," said Vern, "but then I think I'll come back here."

"For what? If you think you're going to get into the pants of Miss-Open-to-the-Universe, you have got another think coming."

"It's not that."

"Then what?"

"I just want to talk to her."

"Talk, talk, what is it with you and women and talk?"

"Lay off, will you?" Vern mumbled.

He drove Neal to the address he'd been given, it was just off the road, a rustic cabin with so many vines and shrubs growing over it, it looked like a mound growing out of the earth. As Neal got out, Vern said, "When should I be back?"

"Don't worry about me, cousin. I can get a ride back with somebody."

"You sure?"

"This is Neal you're talking to, remember?"

Afterward, trying to put together what had happened from this point on, Vern found everything got pretty hazy. He remembered going back, he remembered drinking martinis and, of course, he wasn't used to drinking martinis, maybe that was part of it, but there was also something about this place, the atmosphere of this place, it was so memory-numbing you could get drunk on it alone. He had the sense of having left everything behind, not just the cabin in the Gold Country, but everything that had ever happened to him, he was let loose, he was free.

Right here before him was something huge, he was on the edge of it—the ocean but not just the ocean. . . .

At one point he and the girl and some of the others left the bar and went down a dirt road to the baths. The fog was gone and the stars were sharply bright, even brighter than the Gold Country, with the moon out throwing its light on the water, and the waves crashing below, as if the sound could be some kind of shimmering.

They entered a wooden structure, a place to take off their clothes, all the clothes were put in piles, some neat, some not so neat, he hoped he'd get his own clothes back when the time came to dress, and then you went down into this place, this pool that had a railing in front of it, and faced the sea. It was like a room with three walls.

There was the smell of wetness in rock and in wood. There was the smell of sulfur, the water that came out of the hot spring here had a lot of sulfur in it. The tub was big enough to hold maybe ten, twelve people, if they were close together. And they all got very close together. It was amazing, the girl had said, how when you got people together here, something happened, and she was right.

It was dark in here, you could barely see the others, but it didn't matter, you didn't have to see, you didn't have to know who they were, you were all connected through water, through skin, almost as if skin had become water, and water air, lighter than air. And there was the sound of the waves hitting against the rocks far down below, you couldn't see, but you could hear. He heard someone laugh and say, Water isn't a good lubricant, but he wasn't paying attention, he was thinking, This must be where I always wanted to be.

Following curve after curve on Highway 1 going north, he leaned into each turn, his body loose and easy. If there came the thought of a car going off the road, he saw it suspended above the ocean, floating light as a feather, it never came down. And when he saw the lights of another car coming toward him, it happened twice, they seemed to be not only shining but winking.

He had gone with the girl to her room. There had been great sex. Only, and this was the weird thing, something like erasure was already taking place. He couldn't remember exactly what the girl looked like. Yes she was dark, yes she was slim, but beyond that it was as if she was a person in a dream you'd had but couldn't quite recall. But then he did remember one thing clearly. He remembered a kind of surprise when her cunt had tasted of sulfur, and now he reminded himself that, of course, it was the baths, the baths. And that somehow made it all the more real.

When he got to the city, he knocked on Neal's door, but there was no answer. He got the key from under the mat, and went in. No Neal. Maybe he had stayed over in Big Sur, and if he did, there was no way of knowing whether he'd be back today or tomorrow or even later.

He fell on the couch, broken springs and all, and fell asleep at once.

In the morning, when he woke up, the first thing he smelled was sulfur. It was still there, clinging to the skin of his arm, as if his skin was insisting he remember what he had already forgotten. He sat up and looked around. He noticed how shabby it was in here, for all his cleaning up. And when he looked at the half-painted wall, he felt it was a joke that had gone stale.

He had a weird feeling that this place was doing something to his mind, like what Neal himself could do, jerking him around. He looked at the wall again. He'd been thinking one way, now he was thinking another. Was it because this was Neal's place that he was thinking Neal's thoughts, that he was coming to the definite conclusion that he had been conned, conned by that place, conned by the girl's talk? All that business about free and loose and easy— for some reason he felt shrunk, like he was a balloon that had expanded too fast, and now the air had been let out of him.

He felt an urgent desire to go back to his own place, his own cabin, his own air. Only before he left, he went to the Laundromat and picked up the towels and sheets, and took them back to the pad, where he made up the bed and hung up the towels. As he shut the door, he told himself that at least he left the place cleaner than the way he found it.

CHAPTER

~ 25 ~

AS HE PULLED UP TO HIS CABIN, THE FIRST THING HE
thought was, Finally, I'm back. But when he went into the kitchen
and turned on the overhead light, the things, the O'Keefe and
Merritt stove, the Sears refrigerator, which he'd bought secondhand,
the table he'd made out of a door on two sawhorses, everything told
him he was not back. As if he'd come into somebody else's place. As
if this place had changed in some way when he was gone. As if it
wasn't his anymore.

That happens when you go away, he told himself. That's why it's
better not to go away, to stay where you are.

He opened the refrigerator. He took out two eggs and a salami.
He made himself a salami omelet. It wasn't bad. He consoled himself
with the thought that when he got back into his routine, working
and all, everything would be just as it was, he would be just as he was.

By nine, much earlier than he usually went to bed, he fell into a deep sleep. That is, it started out deep, but soon it was uneasy, a lot of waking up and falling back to sleep, he could hear the sound of his own voice, grating, urgent, trying to get him out of a dream, failing, trying again.

Finally, he awoke.

He got up and went outside. The night was warm. There was a slight breeze, enough to make the leaves tremble, he could just hear the sound of their moving. The moon was shining over the tops of the trees, but it wasn't the same moon he had seen in Big Sur. There was no light shining on the waves, there was no ocean here. He tried to imagine himself back there, to make himself believe he was looking out at the ocean, but the only ocean he could conjure up was the one he looked out on when he was returning from the war. He was on a ship, the war was over, and for days he and his buddies had been sitting on the deck, it was a metal deck, and from all that sitting he couldn't shit, he got terrible piles.

At least he didn't have those anymore. He was regular. Always regular. From his regular life. He had better get back to his regular life.

And indeed after a day, two days, he was back. But then there came a moment: The saw was sawing, the chips were flying, he was bent over, watching closely, careful about his eyes, his fingers, and all of a sudden there was the thought of the girl—not what she looked like, that was getting even vaguer, but the memory of her taste— He told himself to cut it out, to stop it, that was there, this was here.

Later, in the glow of dusk, sitting under his overhang, he reminded himself how much he loved this place, being here alone in this quiet world. The light was fading over the trees, and he heard the night sounds of the forest, he could hear a small animal scrabbling in the brush, and he told himself here he was free to do whatever he wanted to do, no one to tell him anything—it seemed the best place he'd ever had or could have—

But then he thought of that bar and the seminar room, and the baths looking out to sea, and the girl's room afterward, and the more he thought about it the more he decided that place had robbed him of this place, how could that be?

In the morning he decided he was going to go gold panning. He got his gear from the shed and packed it up, adding a few things he kept in a small box in the kitchen: a whisk broom, tweezers, a magnet, and some glass vials. When he was done, he made himself some lunch to take along, a baloney sandwich and an apple, and filled the canteen with water.

He was just about to put the things in the Buick, throw them on top of all that stuff in the back seat, that stuff he'd been carrying around for so long because he couldn't throw any of it out, when he thought, Why do I need all this shit, it's like a weight on my back that I can't get out from under. I'm going to get rid of it all, I'm going to take it to the dump.

Though it was called the dump, it wasn't an official dump. It was just a large, not very deep pit that had been dug a long time ago by miners. People had got into the habit of throwing things into it. You could find old broken chairs and lamps, and even tools. He parked right next to it and got out and just before turning to open the rear door on the driver's side, he saw, among the things that had been flung into the pit, three rubber tires, an old wringer washing machine, and an icebox on its side with its doors flung open, looking as if they were waving. It seemed so sad to him, these things that had once been part of people's lives, now unwanted, useless, replaced with new things, discarded. And he thought, I'm not ready to get rid of anything.

When he got back to the city, he parked in the driveway of the house next door, where there still was no work going on, and went up the stairs of Neal's building to his floor. He knocked and a voice said, "Open sesame."

"It's me, Vern," he said.

Neal was lying on the couch with the torn blanket. "I thought it was someone else. I'm waiting for someone to come by," he said, yawning.

Next to the couch was an old battered suitcase, with a rope around it. "Where you going?"

"I'm splitting, man."

"Yeah, but where?"

"Mexico," he said, but he pronounced it "Muh-hee-co."

"For how long?"

"Six months, a year, maybe longer. . . ."

"To Lila's place?"

"Lila's place?"

"You know, her resort."

"Are you kidding? You think I want to serve time in one of her grass shacks. No, no, I've got other places in mind." Neal yawned again and closed his eyes.

There was something Vern had to say about the place in Big Sur, about the girl, about his own place, about getting conned, about discards. But he didn't say any of that. Instead he said, "You want company?"

"Company?" Neal said, opening his eyes. "You mean you?"

"Yeah, me. I was thinking I might come along. I was thinking I've never seen Mexico. I was thinking it might be fun."

Neal swung himself up so he was sitting straight on the couch. His eyes narrowed. "Cousin," he said, "your idea of fun is not my idea of fun."

"But—"

"Oh no, on this trip I am traveling solo."

"I wouldn't hold you back."

"Your thing—" and here Neal lapsed into a twang, "is not my thing."

Vern laughed to show he could take a joke. He kept telling himself to remember this was just how Neal was, one minute cajoling you and the next minute insulting you, one minute inviting you and the next minute off with one of those somebody elses. He never did remember because as soon as Neal began with his talking and persuading, he ended up saying yes, he couldn't help saying yes.

"Go back, young man, go back. Go back to that cabin of yours with all that peace and quiet, back to your woodcutting and your cooking and your cleaning and your golddigging and your Green Stamps—"

"What's wrong with Green Stamps? You can get a lot of free stuff from them. It's a terrific deal. Every time you buy something you get Green Stamps, and you paste them in the books, and after you fill up enough books, you trade them in. I even got a radio, though there aren't that many stations nearby—"

"Enough," Neal held up his hand, "enough about the Green Stamps."

Vern still wanted to defend the Green Stamps, but was it the Green Stamps or his life he was defending? "Now you're saying, Go back. Before you told me it was a hole, a fucking hole I was living in."

"Did I?"

"First you say one thing and then you say another. It makes me feel no matter what I do you've got something to criticize."

Neal got up from the couch and came over to where Vern was standing and bowed his head. He lifted Vern's right hand and placed it palm down upon his bald pate.

"What the fuck are you doing?"

"My son, I am taking your sins upon my head," Neal intoned.

Vern pushed his hand away. "Cut it out, will you? This isn't funny. You tell me the world's changing, I should go out in the world. So I do that. You tell me to come here, I come here. You tell me to come to a party, I come to a party. You tell me go to Big Sur, I go to Big Sur. What more do you want?"

"Oh, is that it? Well, I'll tell you, after I watched the way you were in Big Sur, lapping up all that shit—"

"I wasn't lapping it up. I was just listening to what she had to say—about changing."

"It's playing mind-games. It has nothing to do with change. With real change."

There's no point in arguing, Vern decided and went over to the sink and looked for a glass but he didn't find a glass, so he turned on the cold water faucet and bent over and drank, and put some of the water in the palm of his hand and wet his face.

"Some people are born gullible," Neal was saying. He was back on the couch again, lying on the torn blanket. "Better they should stay where they are. Who's going to save your ass in the new world? The guy next door? He doesn't give a fuck. Miss Four Eyes? Hardly. She's too wrapped up in finding herself to give a thought to anyone else." Suddenly he grinned slyly, "By the way, did you ever get her in the sack?"

"Well, actually—"

"Light on the fucking, heavy on the talking, I'll bet."

"What are you so mad about?" Vern said.

"Me, mad? How can you say that? I'm mellow, man, mellow."

"What does that mean?"

"I'm easy. I take things as they come. It's the new me. Haven't you noticed? Which is not to say that I don't watch my back. I see how things work, I see how people are. I don't make a big deal of it. And I don't kid myself. What do I do? I rely on my own instincts. Someone else's instincts, are they better than mine? Not by a long shot."

"What if you don't know your own instincts?"

"Then you're in deep shit."

"Neal, this is a bunch of bull. I can tell you don't even believe half of what you're saying."

Neal laughed. "Cousin, you're finally getting the point. The answer is that there is no single answer. You have to keep bobbing and weaving like a good boxer. Do you know, every time I put on my pants in the morning, I do it differently? No one's going to catch me always putting the same leg in my trousers first. The point is to stay one step ahead, to always be on the move, you don't look back, you just keep on—"

There was a knock on the door.

"Well," said Neal, standing and picking up his suitcase by the rope, "I'm on my way, ready to open myself to the universe. You know, the thought has occurred to me, I could probably do something like that, run a seminar, put people together, and see what happens. That would be some fucking seminar. In fact, it could be a seminar on fucking. Think of all the different kinds of fucks there are," and he began to list them off on his fingers, "a fighting fuck, a boring fuck, a scary fuck, a desperate fuck, a funny fuck, you could try them all out—"

He started out the door and then turned back. "You can stay here tonight if you feel like it. After tonight, it's rented for the duration. Don't look so gloomy, man. The way I see it, if you're meant to risk, you risk, if not, not." And with those words, he was out the door.

Vern sat on the torn blanket on the torn couch for a long time, trying to think what he should do. Neal had said he should go back. But how could you trust anything he said? Whatever he said one moment was different the next. Just when you thought he was being straight with you, he made it clear he was having you on. And then in the moment after that, he was saying something different, entirely opposite. Like there was a whole succession of Neals, a whole set of beings, always another one hiding behind the one you were seeing. It made Vern feel dumb, as well as oddly naked, as if he himself had nothing to hide behind, but then what did he have to hide?

He remembered how his mother had said to watch out for Neal, he was a bad influence, she kept warning him that Neal was going to get him in trouble if he wasn't careful. The more he thought of what she said, the madder he got, but he couldn't tell if he was mad at her or at Neal.

As he sat on the couch, the light—what little light there was in the room—began to fade. He heard a kind of throaty, clucking sound from the window, and he got up, and there on the windowsill, which looked out on an air shaft, was a pigeon, gray and white with beady eyes. Startled at his approach, the pigeon beat its wings and flew away.

He sat in the chair again and waited for something in the room to give him an order, a direction. He looked at the torn rug, at the bed, no doubt with dirty sheets by this time, at the painted wall with its uneasy edge between the red and the tan.

The room was saying, Stay. Rooms say that, he knew. They have to stay, so they want you to stay. The thought of his place, his own place, was bitter. It had become a prison to remind him of who he no longer was.

He heard the pigeon on the sill again. He went to the refrigerator and found an old crust of bread. He opened the window wide and the pigeon flew off. He broke the crust into pieces and put them on the sill. Maybe it will come back, he thought, closing the window.

Faint noises were coming from the street—an engine gunning, a horn sounding, a siren in the distance—outside, in the city, all those people were doing what they were doing, working, playing, walking, running, eating, drinking, and here he was, sitting inside, a lump on a sofa. Neal had said, You need to get out in the world, but he had only gotten out partway, and now Neal was all for shoving him back in again.

But he couldn't blame Neal.

He had put himself in a hole. He had stayed there. In some way, all along he had been—he was—a loser.

He thought of the girl in the baths, and of being in the pool with the other people, not knowing them, but being with them just the same. And there was a longing in him here in the city with all the unknown people out there, and he in this room alone, a longing to be part of their life, he in their life, no different from them.

What if—a thought came—his thought or not his thought—what if every room was open to everybody, or anybody? So when you got up in the morning, you went out and left your room, but in the evening you came back to any room you wanted, and there was a person in the room waiting, but nobody was anybody's special person, everybody was everybody's person, every room was everybody else's room.

188 | MILLICENT DILLON

He heard a phone ringing, it had to be the pay phone in the hall-way. It rang and rang, and stopped. It started again.

At that moment he thought of Edmond—Edmond whom he had not seen or heard from for so long, Edmond who had admired his place and talked about his wonderful life, Edmond who said he would go gold panning with him someday but he never did go, never did get in touch with him.

He thought of the girl who was with Edmond—her first name began with an L, no, not Lila, Lorle, yes, that was it—but what was her last name? It would come to him, he should just not try to think of it too hard, after a while it would come.

He heard the pigeon again. It had come back to the sill. He turned and saw it pecking away at the crumbs he'd put there. It gobbled them all up fast, its head bobbing, as it balanced on its spindly orange-red claws, holding fast to the sill. He wasn't sure that it was the same pigeon as before.

ᴄ 26 ᴐ

IN THE ROOM EACH CHILD IS SEPARATE FROM EVERY OTHER child. One girl is sitting on the floor, rocking. Above her, the shade of an overhead light has been dislodged, so the bulb is hanging bare. She reaches with one arm up toward the light, and utters a high birdlike cry. Slowly she lowers her arm and subsides into rocking. A moment later, she reaches toward the light, crying out.

A boy is jumping on a stack of inflated inner tubes. His jumps seem measured, each one calibrated to be the same height as the one before. He stares into the distance, as if he is seeking a single point to guarantee the accuracy of his going up and his coming down.

A girl is pacing off a geometric pattern on the asphalt tile floor. She steps forward with her right foot, then moves her left up to it, steps to the right with her right foot, then moves her left sideways to it, moves her right foot back a step, then brings her left foot to it, steps to the left with her left foot, then moves her right to it. Returned to her starting point, she stops and says, "It is a fire of circles. I shall never see Heaven again."

Then she repeats the pattern again. . . .

Though these motions are repetitive, they do not seem mechanical. Or so Lorle thinks, watching the children, on this, her first day as a volunteer at the Children's Center. Each movement seems a statement, if not to others, then to the one who is moving. Each repetition, in other words, purposeful.

Of course she may just be reading into their minds, into their intentions, the workings of her own.

For she too has her repetitions, though hers are not of motion, but of words and images, the same over and over again.

As now:

It is Saturday evening. It is five o'clock. She has been waiting to hear from him. Four days ago she gave him an ultimatum. This is the last day. Yes, she still feels intense desire for him, how could she not, but isn't there also the will, if not the desire, to be free of him. Even as she says to herself, Stick to what you told him, she can't help waiting for the phone to ring. It is still Saturday, there is still time.

Soon she must call Joan to send Julie home. She has been over there since early afternoon, playing with Joan's daughter, Carrie. She opens the door, she goes outside, the local evening paper lies on the lawn. She picks it up, takes off the rubber band that binds it, and stretches the band around her fingers. She goes inside and closes the door. She has left the door open in case the phone rings. The phone has not rung. She sits at the kitchen table.

(On the front page there was a headline. What was it?)

She turns the page, and on the second page, halfway down, in small headlines, his name seized her, joined to another word, "dies."

Beneath these words, other words dissolve and reassemble:

". . . 45-year-old physician . . . found dead in bed last night . . . body was found by his wife, Carol . . . death apparently caused by a heart attack."

She reads the words again.

They are the same as what she has read.

She is on the edge between before and after. The knowledge after. . . . The absence of knowledge before. . . .

She tells herself she must be clear about sequence. Otherwise—

She does not know what "otherwise" entails but surely it has to do with surviving what follows.

Days follow—weeks follow—months have followed—haven't they?

One step forward, one step back, two steps forward, two steps back. . . .

As now:

It is Saturday evening. It is five o'clock. She has been waiting to hear from him, waiting not to hear from him. Four days ago she gave him an ultimatum. It is the last day. . . .

She has been told simply to observe on this, her first day. She sees Janet, the girl who is making the square pattern on the floor, suddenly stop. She sees her turn and walk toward where she is standing. She stops about four feet away. Her head is bent, she seems to be studying the floor. She says, almost inaudibly, "You make me think of the grave." She returns to her place in the room, to her starting point, and begins her pattern again.

Yes, she is right, I make myself think of the grave, of the grave in the cemetery, where his body lies in a casket decaying, even as I must go back to my starting point, to:

It is Saturday evening. It is five o'clock. I have been waiting to hear from him. . . .

Yet here is an odd thing, which she notes in passing in this room that is like a way station for repetitions: She cannot repeat her old pattern of anxiety. Where has it gone? Perhaps it has simply been replaced, parceled out into fragments, so that when she looks at any child in this room she thinks she sees anxiety in a jump, a cry, a repeated movement of a foot upon the floor.

Being here is like being in a dream, subject to interpretation, object of interpretation.

She is standing watching Klaus, the boy who jumps on the inflated inner tubes. She must try to stop him. She throws over him a huge red net that is semitransparent. Through the net his face is barely recognizable. His nose is flattened out, as it presses against the redness. His eyes are red holes. He wraps the netting more tightly around himself and climbs into the hole at the center of the inner tubes. But now she sees he is falling, falling faster and faster, and she throws herself into the hole after him to save him.

And a thought comes on awaking: In dreams everything is its opposite, wasn't that one of Freud's statements?

She has decided she must no longer rely on the words of others. She will no longer be the one who went to the library in search of understanding, who made extensive notes on what she read, transcribing exact words and passages on body image, on movement, on transference, as if by copying them, the words would somehow become her own. Now, if she looks at the pages of that notebook into which she copied those words, she feels contempt for the one who did the copying, for the one who thought she would find understanding that way.

But then, perhaps the impulse to copy has just taken another form: repetition, the repeating of a primal scene, primal in that it is strictly limited to itself and nothing more, no interpretation required.

It is Saturday evening. It is five o'clock. I have been waiting. . . .

She dreams of leaving. Only when she is far away does she remember that she has left Julie alone in the house. She is aghast at her forgetfulness. She returns home to find the house is full of police, who accuse her, What kind of a mother are you? How could you leave this child alone? She tells them that Julie is much older than she seems, she can take care of herself. When the police leave, she hits Julie across the face. What have you done? Why did you call them? she screams. You have ruined me, you have made me a criminal in their eyes. Yet she cannot rid herself of the sensation of the stinging of the palm of her hand with which she hit her, she cannot stop seeing the look of fear in the child's eyes.

For the time being—that is how she puts it to herself—a strange phrase, that time has being—she has agreed to Julie staying with Michael and Edith, his new wife. (He has slipped so quickly, so easily into a new marriage.) She tells herself that it is better for Julie not to have to be with her. She tells herself that it will only be for the summer. Yet once the responsibility for care of the child is no longer hers, she feels abandoned.

As for the children at the center, she does not feel motherly toward them. She does not quite know what she feels except that she is on an equal plane with them.

She has come to believe that they—each one of them—have two lives at the same time. A stopped life and a life that strives by repetition to be continuous. As does she. This gives to each of their movements a strange and unnerving quality of constantly starting and stopping and starting again—like her movements, her thoughts, the movement of her thoughts—

As now:

It is Saturday evening. It is five o'clock. I have been waiting. . . .

At the moment of his dying, would he have thought of her? No, she does not think so.

She does not know what he would have been thinking of. She did not know him, that she knows. She never knew him, no wonder she

could not call him by his name, he was a generic being, a represen-
tation, there was always in her relation to him awe, as if he was—had
been—is a sacred being.

She is standing beside John, the biggest child in the room. He is sitting in a chair, holding a stack of scratched and worn records in his
hands. He is nodding his head to the rhythm of the song he seems to
be hearing. He drops his right hand down and makes a thumping
noise, then puts the top record on the bottom of the stack. With
another record on the top, he says, "The Donut Song," and nods his
head back and forth to the rhythm of the one song he is always playing, always listening to. And when he speaks, he speaks in numbers,
of 45 rpm records, of 33 rpm records, of 78 rpm records.

She goes up the path to her house, she takes out her key, she opens
the door. Everything is in place but there is no safety here, no comfort. She should have left long ago. She waited too long. She cannot leave now. She is imprisoned by his dying, which is not yet a
death.

She has taken out of the closet the crimson silk shirt she was wearing when he sat on the couch with her, when he spoke of seeing her
sweat. She thinks there is something not right with this shirt, or is it
her body that is at fault? It should be looser, she should be thinner.
She can open the seams, the seams are generous, there will be a lot of
room left in the fabric if she opens them. She picks at the stitches of
the seam with a tool with a curved hook. The stitches are so tight,

each one must be laboriously picked at. She falls into a small frenzy at all the time this is taking. If I cut the seam—

She cuts.

She has ruined the shirt.

She is watching Mary, the girl who rocks on the floor, who over and over again strives to reach the bare bulb above her, crying out. Watching her, she thinks about distance, about calculating distance with one's eyes, distances that can and cannot be overcome. Does one learn to do this, beginning with infancy, or is it part of the structure of the brain, to be able to estimate distance from an object, a being? To know, at each point, as one moves toward one's goal, how much farther one has to go to reach the end point. But is it possible in Mary that the only sense of distance she has is one that cannot be overcome? Or is there something about the light— like a sun, a symbol—that she wants to go toward, and wants not to reach?

She was a child, about to fall asleep. There was a dim light in the room, from a neighbor, from the moon. She could see the corner of the room, where two walls met below the ceiling. The walls, the corner, began to move, no, she could detect no movement, but there had been movement so now everything was farther away. The ordinary judgment made with one's eyes about distance no longer applied in this room she knew so well. She felt terror at the thought that she could not know what was near and what was far. When she cried out, her mother came into the room, and switched on the light. In that light, she, her face, was at a distance, far away; it did not help that she knew she was near.

It has all had to do with eyes.

At night, lying in bed, she stares into a corner. Will it return, the never repressed? Though she no longer remembers his eyes, it is as if his eyes have been implanted in hers, so she sees only what he would have her see, a vast interior landscape—

One could get lost in that infinite interior.

Is this madness? No, this is not madness. Madness could not be so unforgiving.

She is simply back to her old devices, caught between the rapid dodges of her inner life, and the world beyond her skin, caught between fear and the fear of being taken over by fear, a relentless shifting of belief.

Hysteria—anxiety hysteria—her diagnosis—her case—

Hysteria—from the Greek, *hystera*; the womb, a disease of the womb, the Greeks thought

But isn't a hysteric supposed to be someone shrieking, raving, but weren't there also some who were inert, paralyzed, those late-nineteenth- or early-twentieth-century women, patients of Freud's, suffering from a disease he connected with the repression of sexual thoughts, feelings, experiences?

She is not raving, but she is inert.

I hope you don't mind my dropping by like this, Patricia says. You're not answering your phone, or is your phone out of order?

No, it's working.

I haven't heard from you, I was beginning to wonder. . . .

I've been busy.

You are so thin. Well, it's not surprising, after a divorce one gets thinner—or fatter.

I am the same as I was.

She does not want to invite Patricia in. She invites her in. She manages to carry on a conversation, though it is no more than an imitation of a conversation.

Maybe imitation is hysteria. Maybe hysteria is imitation. The need to give things a form—to rule out uncreated form.

Now Patricia is telling about her lover. Or, no, she is talking about two lovers. She is going to go up to the city to meet the new one this week. She says, It just occurred to me. My old lover is going to be here this week too. I can't go. He's very nice. Maybe you'd like to—

Like to—?

Go up and meet him.

To go as a substitute?

Not exactly as a substitute, no.

Sort of.

So then if I should be a substitute for her, what would I do? I would go to the city. I would knock on the door. He would open the door. I would say—what? I am here, for sex.

No, I don't think so.

If you change your mind, here's his number, at the hotel.

A piece of paper with a number on it.

He once gave her a piece of paper with a number on it.

I should call Craig, she thinks. He helped me before. But she does not call him, she cannot get herself to call him.

She has been asked to help get the children to form a circle. Most of them resist, insisting on being left to their own motions, but a few are persuaded to arrange themselves unevenly around a center. The teacher puts a record on the record player.

"You put your right foot in, you put your right foot out, you put your right foot in and you shake it all about, you do the hokey-pokey and you turn yourself around, that's what it's all about. . . .

"You put your left foot in. . . .

"You put your right hand in. . . .

"You put your left hand in. . . .

"You put your head in. . . . you put your head out. . . .

Janet, who has been watching from off to the side, drops her head forward and backward. She stops and cries out, "I'm afraid it will fall off."

Up to now, there has always been in her a belief in motion, in life as motion.

Now, she is stopped.

Now that she is wholly in this grief, her motion has no force.

Was it love, or only—only?—transference love?

Love that began in a frame, framed by a hope, a need, framed by an agreement, framed by payment for services. She paid, or rather the insurance company paid. He was paid. It was all defined in the world, by the world.

Then the frame was shattered.

After which the love became, not an exemplary one ("I told you I'd fuck you, you bitch"), but one that was primitive, unevolved, with no social force and limitation, no framing at all.

But now that he is dead, death is the frame.

And she is more tightly bound to him than ever.

At night she hears a knocking on the door. It is an urgent knocking, signaling danger. She jumps out of bed and runs to the door. She opens it. There is no one there. She goes out into the street barefoot. There is no one there.

She turns on the light, she turns on all the lights. She goes from room to room.

She sees on the shelf (Is it chance, or was she looking for it?) the book by Wilhelm Reich. She takes it off the shelf. She opens it to the chapter "Emotional Plague."

The term "emotional plague" has no defamatory connotation. . . . The individual afflicted with the emotional plague *limps, characterologically speaking. The emotional plague is a chronic biopathy of the organism.*

She closes the book. She puts it back on the shelf.

It is the wrong book. What is the right book?

The book of risk—the book of all that was gained, now lost—the book about the Gold Country . . . about a dog howling . . . about the car stopping . . . stopping . . . about walking . . . about a letter . . . about a man running. . . .

She is being bound by plot.

It is Saturday evening. . . .

Yet everything is by chance.

Sequence is by chance.

If not this, then that. . . .

It is Saturday evening. . . .

She thinks of how a melody begins, it goes on, through many repetitions to its necessary ending. And when you remember the melody
in your mind, it begins, it continues, but finally it stops. A melody of
memory beginning and ending.

It is Saturday afternoon.
There is a knock on the door.

↶ 27 ↷

WHEN SHE OPENED THE DOOR, A MAN STOOD BEFORE HER. What is he selling? she wondered. He did not seem like a salesman.

"Do you—" he stopped. "Do you—uh—remember me?"

Hearing his voice, that voice with the slight twang, she thought she recognized him, though even then she hesitated.

"It's me, Vern." He looked down, his shoulders gave a slight shrug.

"How are you?" she asked.

He looked tired, he looked worn.

"Fine, thank you. I hope you don't mind my coming knocking on your door this way. . . ."

"But how did you know where I live?"

"I looked your name up in the phone book."

"Oh," she said, uneasily.

"I hope I'm not interrupting. I wouldn't want to interrupt."

"No, you're not interrupting."

She led him into the living room, he sat on the couch, she asked him if he'd like something to drink. Coffee, tea, a beer?

"If it's no bother," he said.

"It's no bother."

"Coffee. Thank you."

Everything had been surprising from the moment she opened the door. She was dark, she was slim. She could have been the girl in Big Sur. She was so like her, almost like her. But of course she wasn't her.

And now when she came in with the coffee he was even more confused, the way she moved, so quickly, the way she was abrupt and shy at the same time, the way she was so . . . he didn't have a word for it—the way she stared at him with her dark eyes, not smiling, wounded somehow, like an animal at bay. That wasn't like the girl in Big Sur.

She put the coffee down on the table in front of him. She sat in a kind of canvas chair you would think would be an outdoor chair. He saw she was waiting for him to say something but he didn't know what to say. He picked up the cup and drank. The coffee seemed bitter to him. He swallowed hard and put the cup down on the table. He had the sense that he was losing hold of what he was doing here, why he had come here to this house with all this glass, a whole wall of glass, too open to view.

"I was looking for Edmond, Dr. Edmond, and I couldn't find him and I thought maybe you'd know where he is."

She turned away and looked out of the floor-to-ceiling window onto the outside greenness, onto the eucalyptus trees, whose leaves were moving in the breeze, not as in a dream she'd once had, in which the trees had been cut down, cut off at their roots, there were no branches, no leaves. She turned back and looked at Vern and for a moment she was afraid that he was going to recede into the distance.

"He"—and here she hesitated, but she was reassured, for he was still where he should be, on the couch, a few feet from her—"he died."

"He died? When?"

When did he die? It had to have been—

"Last year. He died last year. No, over a year ago."

That had to be so, weeks had passed, months had passed, she had marked their passing day to day, each day an unbelievably ordinary day—in that she couldn't believe it ordinary—

"I'm real sorry to hear that." After a moment, he asked, "What did he die of?"

"They said it was a heart attack."

She did not know how she could be saying these words, so calmly, so simply, when up to now she had been unable to talk to anyone about him. Yet now, just now, she had said them to this man, Vern, who hardly knew him, but this too was true, he had been with the two of them . . . on that trip . . . in his car. . . .

"He was a young man," he said. "He looked so strong."

"Yes, just forty-five," she said.

"That's still young."

She had never thought of him as young or old. She had never thought of him as a particular age until he died, but there it was in the paper, forty-five.

"He"—he shook his head—"he said one time he wanted to go gold panning."

"He said he wanted to go?"

"He said it would be a good way to take his mind off his work, our going and doing the gold panning together."

Together?

She thought of all that Edmond and she could not do and had not done together.

"I thought this was a good time, there's still water, the streams are still full enough of water, we had a rainy winter—"

In the silence that followed she was thinking of other silences, her silences and Edmond's silences when she had been his patient. How agonizing those silences had been to her. You were supposed to say what came to your mind—and often nothing came to her mind—and he of course called it resistance, and when she denied it he spoke of repression, and she would finally find words, and he would take them for clues to the repressed. And he would interpret, and she, convinced, would seize upon his interpretations as the key, the answer. . . .

There was something about silence, she now thought—she had not thought about this before—that was basic, rudimentary, that linked inside to outside. In it one became even more open to sound, as now she heard the refrigerator come on in its usually unheard cycle. And outside, from the street, the sound of a car passing, the shout of a child at play, muted sounds and not so muted sounds, the sound of drumming from the boy who lived two doors down. . . .

And another sound, on the other side of silence, wondrous when she heard it, now almost like a tolling. . . .

She was sitting in his outer office, a very small room with two doors, two straight chairs, a window looking out upon a light well, a small table holding a plant with stiff leaves. (Trying to get every detail right was like forcing her way through a thicket.) This was to be her last session, or so she had decided. And then she was in his inner office, where she had said to him—she had spoken the words—it was her voicing but of words that had taken their cue from him— For many days she had been picking up from him a sense of his intense response to her—not said outright but conveyed by errors—Freudian slips— which he himself had taught her how to interpret—

Yet she was the one who spoke the words.

The words had come from her, or from him through her, or from the situation itself—the two of them alone in the room— She had not even (she thinks now) planned to say them. They had just erupted, a surge of something held back for too long, suddenly released.

A release following upon another release.

Some time before she had broken with Michael, told him she wanted out of the marriage, told him whatever arrangements he wanted to make would be agreeable with her. She was not angry, not demanding, there were no recriminations. She just wanted it over. She had waited a long time to say the words.

And now with him, too, she would say what she had to say: Now that I will no longer be your patient, I wanted to say to you that I would be—available.

There was a long silence after that. He did not say, Thanks but no thanks. He could have but he did not. And there was the evidence before her, in the way he looked at her, in his bodily posture as well, that he would not. Yes, she could read his body, or so she thought then.

(No, she had not been lying down, she had been sitting up, facing him, as she now faced Vern.)

"I will think about it and let you know next time."

Wasn't that what he had said?

How was it possible that she could have forgotten the exact words? She had thought they were permanently imprinted on her brain. Hadn't Freud said that nothing was ever really forgotten? Was that so or was it not so?

What was memory telling her?

Not enough, maybe too much, about the next session, the actual last session, as she was waiting in his waiting room, waiting to go into his office, to hear what he would say. Waiting for him to open the door to his consulting room, she heard a sound in the silence. It was, she realized, a vibration in the wall, from the other side of the wall. What could it be from, this sudden buzzing?

Then it came to her what it must be. There was a little bathroom off his consulting room. And the wall of that room shared a common wall with the wall of this little waiting room. And the sound, she recognized it—it was the vibration of an electric razor.

With that sound she knew she had won, or felt she had won, although now she could not say whether she had won or lost. Still, she held to the sound, clinging to it as it retreated, reaching toward it as it died away.

And for one moment this room—its structure and its furnishings, the glass wall, the wooden walls, that couch on which Vern was sitting, this canvas chair—it too vibrated.

"He was," Vern said suddenly in the silence, "a good man."

Vern was used to silence, he was often silent with others, but this silence was going on too long. So he had said that about his being a good man. And in the saying of it he felt sorrow. He had hardly known Edmond, had only seen him twice. Yet he believed what he said was true.

She kept looking at him, those staring eyes again, and she didn't say anything.

"But he was in some kind of trouble, I knew that, I could see that."

"Did he tell you he was in trouble?"

"No, he didn't say but I could tell from the way he was talking at my place about my life being so peaceful, that his own life was not peaceful."

"Peaceful?"

"Not peaceful."

She remembered what he had said about peace after she had cursed him, yes, she had cursed him, she must have been half mad, hysterical, but curses can't do anything, they are just words.

"I thought maybe it had something to do with his being in the war, with what had happened in the war."

"He was in the war?"

"He was a lieutenant or maybe a captain in the Army."

"He told you that?"

She felt a sudden spasm of jealousy. Why should you be jealous? she reproached herself. It is the kind of thing that men tell men. She could count up on one hand all the things that he had told her, while she had told him everything—well, almost everything. But who ever said that telling was supposed to be counted? "What else did he say?"

"About what?"

"About the war?"

"He didn't say anything else about the war. I could be wrong, maybe it wasn't about the war—"

He had said too much, said the wrong thing to her, what was the right thing? He could feel himself becoming cautious, not wanting to upset her. Yet there was a cowardice in being too cautious, as if you'd given up even before you began. He remembered what Neal had said: If you're meant to risk, you risk, if not, not.

"Have you ever been to Big Sur?" he risked.

"To Big Sur? To Big Sur," she repeated the words, as if she was evaluating them. "Yes, why?"

"I was just wondering."

"Just once. A couple of years ago. We went camping in the state park."

"You like to go camping?"

"Not much. I get cold. I got cold." She laughed, a little. "Do you want some more coffee?"

"No, thanks, I'm fine with this."

But he didn't feel fine. He felt uncomfortable—no, not so much uncomfortable as uneasy, unable to compel his face to withhold, to protect him from outside eyes.

"It sure is beautiful," he said loudly.

"Beautiful?"

"In Big Sur."

"Yes."

In the silence that followed she thought she heard a meowing at the front door, Julie's cat wanting to come in. But then the meowing stopped.

"I was just in Big Sur."

"Did you go to the park?"

"No, not the park. We went to this place, where people come for seminars, you go for a weekend, you can do that, we didn't do that, we just stopped by."

"Oh?" she said.

She was thinking about the time they went camping at Big Sur, and one day they went to the ocean, and Michael showed her fossils in the cliffs that were millions of years old—or were they hundreds of millions of years?—Michael who loved everything to do with rocks, with geological time, and thinking of how he got so excited about such things, suddenly she remembered how she had loved that in him. She hadn't thought about loving him for a long time.

Vern was remembering the words of the girl at Big Sur. What she looked like was hazy, except for her being dark and slim, but the words she said had stayed with him for all that Neal had mocked them.

"The important thing, they said," he said, embarrassed at his own saying, yet he pushed on, "is to say what you feel, to—to express yourself, who you really are."

"Who said that?"

"The people at the seminar at Big Sur I was telling you about."

"Oh?" she said.

"Maybe it's because of that place, it being so far away from everything you're used to, and that's all you do the whole weekend, you're with the other people in the seminar, and you keep on talking—"

"Talking?"

"Talking, and other things."

What was it about her, about this place, about being here—why was he here?—that made him feel he must take their side, stake their claim?

"They go there to change their lives. They say that after one seminar their whole life changes."

"One weekend doesn't seem like a lot of time to change your whole life around."

"That's what they told me."

"I thought you didn't like change," she said.

"What makes you say that?"

"I remember. You said it in the car."

"Did I? You have a real good memory."

"Only for some things," she said. She turned and looked out the glass wall.

He saw he was losing her. It bothered him a lot, but the strange thing was that in this room where you could see all the greenness through the glass, the plants were waving in the breeze like plants waving underwater, and it was getting all mixed up, this room and the pool in his mind. . . .

So he told her about the pool, how people got into the pool, into the hot spring water, and how it was built into a cliff out over the ocean, you and all the others, so close together in the pool—

"A swimming pool?"

"Too small for swimming, you're not swimming, you're just standing in it, and the air is cool, and the water is very warm." He wanted to tell her what it was like without clothes, to feel your skin against the skin of the other who was like her but wasn't her.

Though it was almost dark by now, she had not yet turned on a light. Sitting across from him, seeing only his vague outline, she became aware of his desire for her. In the almost darkness she thought of his eyes, which she could not now see, and remembered what she had thought when she was riding in the car with him, that they were hungry, too eager.

Where is the cat? she wondered, Julie's cat. I thought I heard her at the front door. I promised Julie I would take care of her. Every time I talk to her on the phone she wants to know, Did I feed her? Did I let her come in at night?

She got up and turned on the light, and opened the front door but the cat wasn't there. She opened the sliding glass door to the patio, and called, "Bailey!" and Bailey came in and ran into the kitchen. She followed her, and took out a can of cat food from the cupboard above the sink. While she was stooped down, spooning out half the can into Bailey's dish, Vern came in carrying his cup, and put it on the counter.

"Well, I guess I'd best be going, I'm sure you have things to do," he said.

Still stooped, she felt the first stirrings of something like desire, not like the desire she felt for Edmond, so overwhelming and encompassing, but rather a skewed desire—as if aimed at one, arriving at another.

"There's this place in Mexico. I'm thinking of driving down there," he said suddenly.

She stood up. Her eyes, he saw, were changed, not staring, startled.

He started telling her about the Villa of Peace, telling her that it was a kind of a paradise, and so cheap. Remembering the words that were on the paper, he told her it was a place where you could get away from everything, a peaceful place, where there was never a harsh word.

She felt the cat brush against her shin, its back arched. She saw that the food was gone. Should she give her some more?

She was only supposed to have half a can at night, half in the morning.

"I was wondering—if you—if you—would like to—maybe—"

She was bent down on her haunches, spooning out the rest of the food into the cat's dish.

"—go with me."

The cat brushed by her again.

"Go with you where?"

"To that place I was telling you about in Mexico that's like—that's like a kind of paradise—

"Paradise?"

The cat purred, as if in appreciation.

"Well," he said, "not really. It's somebody's idea of a paradise."

She stood up. "You're asking me to go with you? Why?"

He flushed. "I just thought—maybe—you seemed—it might do you some good, it might help—"

"You think I need help?"

The cat was gulping down the food.

"I don't know. I just thought—"

Looking at him, she felt a sense of panic. I do need help, she wanted to say, but is it the kind of help you can give me? She pulled herself up sharply. She took a deep breath.

"Have you been there?"

"No, never."

"Then how do you know what it's like?"

"I read about it."

"In a guidebook?"

"No, in some papers someone gave me."

She was leaping from one weird thing together with him, yet at the same time she reassured herself, There is something very simple about this, even ordinary, somehow. What is ordinary? Normal, regular, everyday, but of course it's crazy, it's not everyday, it's—

All of which led suddenly to a longing in her, a longing for ordinariness and maybe even a happy ending or at least an ending happier than the one she had come to. She felt a sob arising, a sob in her throat. And yet almost at once there was that in her bitterly condemning this display as sentimental. But what if that's what I want, what I need?

The cat was meowing at the front door, waiting to be let out. She went to the door and opened it; the cat scampered out. When she came back into the kitchen, she saw him standing there, waiting, leaning against the counter. What did she know about him? Practically nothing. She had seen him only once before this. Was he a good man? What was a good man? How could she decide? Ask him for references? Not likely.

The first time she saw Edmond she didn't know who he was.

She saw him from across the street. A door closed behind him, he stepped out on the landing, followed the path to the sidewalk and then made a left turn—a right turn to her, as she was on the other side of the street, waiting to cross. She saw a tall well-built man in a blue suit, striding forward with his head held high. Still she noticed, she could not help noticing even from across the street that there was an oddity in his walking, an almost imperceptible twist, a rolling so slight it could not have been voluntary. She felt that twisting, that rolling in her own body, like a stab of recognition, like a capitulation to secrecy.

She had had enough of secrecy.

"How many days are you talking about?" she asked him.

He swallowed.

"Five or six days, maybe a week—"

"I have to be back by Labor Day." Julie would be back by then. Public school would start right afterward, and she would have to be available for her new job as a substitute teacher.

"We'd be sure to be back by then."

She looked around the room, checking to see what was and wasn't in place. "I couldn't go right away. I have things to take care of."

"You could fly down to Mexico City when you're ready, and I'll meet you there, and you could fly back."

"I just don't know," she said.

"I'll get you a ticket. I don't mean for you to pay. I'm the one asking you to go. I'd be glad for the company."

And then she shrugged. "I'll think it over. Call me tomorrow and I'll let you know."

After she closed the door behind him, she stood in the entryway. The cat had come back in again, and now she wanted to go out again. The cat sashayed against her leg. She let the cat out.

You're out of your mind, she said to herself.

You know nothing about this man.

But what did she ever know about Edmond except what she made up?

You know nothing about this place you're going to.

All she could remember was that he said it was a place with "never a harsh word," a phrase that sounded as if it was lifted from an old song. What was it?

". . . where seldom is heard a discouraging word and the skies are not cloudy all day."

She hummed the song to its ending.

Discouraging, not harsh, she thought, and laughed harshly.

I'll never go, that's crazy, a man comes in here, and just like that—just like that—you listen to his words—and without knowing what you're doing, why you're doing it—you're ready to risk—

For what?

Certainly not for love.

Then for what?

For sex?

Why with him and not somebody else?

Maybe because there's a kind of naïveté in him, a kind of innocence—

Maybe because he came, maybe because he's here, maybe because he asked.

It is Saturday evening. . . .

I would think you've had enough risk.

It is Saturday evening. . .

And what about the risk in repetition, in a foreshortened history of desire, of need, felt and half fulfilled, with gaps and sudden disclosures?

It is Saturday evening. . . .

Let it go.

Let him go.

You are going. You are going to Mexico.

Yes, I'm going, she told herself, with a determination as fierce as rage, but rage laced with grief, every cell of her body lamenting loss, rage, loss.

It was Saturday evening. . . .

The memory was a spasm.

A sudden and violent involuntary muscular contraction, as of a convulsive or painful nature.

A sudden, violent, convulsive movement.

IT IS TWO O'CLOCK IN THE MORNING IN ROOM 623 IN THE
Hotel Guardiola in Mexico City.

There is repetition here, after all.

Sex has been repeated, four, five, six times, she has lost count.

There is the smell of it, the sweat of it, in this bed with this man
whose body naked or clothed until this night has been strange to
her.

What is not here:

There is no reverie.

There is no hopeless hoping.

There is none of the slow waiting, the weight of romanticism, the
leading up to something, after delay and delay and delay. There is the
simplest of timing: immediacy.

There is only body to fall into, movement and response: kissing, holding, stroking, tightening, loosening, licking, sucking, entering, being entered until one is, almost, besotted with desire.

He sleeps, she sleeps. He awakes, she awakes.

They begin again.

He sleeps, she sleeps. She awakes. It is still dark. Through the window a shaft of light is being thrown upon the floor. She gets up and opens the window. Looking up, she can see the moon shining, pale, remote. Across the court activity is taking place in a room, it may be a laundry room. Some kind of machine is going, a light has been lit, there are voices.

She goes back to bed. He is sleeping deeply.

A thought comes to her of what else is not here: there is no smell of mold, only the faintest smell of sweat, and now coming from across the way, the smell of laundry, of huge vats, of boiling water, of soap, a cleansing smell.

She falls into a dreamless sleep.

After she got off the plane and went through customs, she looked for him but she did not see him. Then a man in the waiting crowd smiled and waved. It was Vern. He looked different somehow, she had thought him smaller. He was taller, thinner, his coloring no longer faded, but surprisingly vivid.

But his car was still the same, the backseat piled high with things. He put her suitcase in the trunk.

As they drove toward the center of the city in the darkness, he told her that there was a problem, the Villa was closed for a day or two, they couldn't take any guests, but he was supposed to call back tomorrow.

"So then what will we do?"

"Do?" He was concentrating on the road ahead, just as he had when he was driving in the Gold Country, though that road was nothing like this road.

"We can stay here. There's lots to see. Is that okay with you?"

"We'll be tourists," she said, and laughed.

A substitute teacher on a substitute trip, why not a substitute itinerary?

They are having breakfast at Sanborn's. She has bought a *Guide to Mexico City* in the bookshop. If they are to be tourists, at least they can do it systematically. The guide lists tours, restaurants, hotels, best places to shop. On the first page are facts about the city: "Situated in a valley between the peaks of the Sierra Nevada, 7349 feet above sea level. . . ." She skips over other facts—the population, the weather. . . .

"When the Aztecs came to the valley of Mexico in 1325 or so," she reads out loud, "the head priest saw a vision of a royal eagle with a serpent in its mouth—"

"Let's go back to the room after breakfast," he says.

Shortly they are back in bed.

He seizes her in a frenzy of desire. He needs to have her now, this instant, he can't wait. The taste of her cunt is not the same as the taste of the girl in Big Sur. There is no sulfur here. He has never known anything like this. To do it to her, to feel her feeling it being done to her—and then to enter.

"Let's go out," she says. "We really should go out."

"But it's so nice here." He nuzzles against her. "Where do you want to go?"

"I'll look in the guidebook."

She gets out of bed and goes over to the dresser, but at the moment she reaches for the guidebook, she has to put her hand out on the dresser to steady herself.

"Are you all right?" he asks her.

"Just for a moment I felt dizzy."

"You have to be careful here the first few days, because of the altitude."

"I'm all right," she says, though even as she says this, she thinks, Am I pushing myself too far, too fast?

She turns the pages of the guidebook. "The museum, the Museum of Anthropology, let's go to the museum."

"'The Calendar Stone' or 'Stone of the Sun' is a circular disc carved of basalt and weighs 22 tons. It was found near the Zócalo during excavation in December, 1790.

"The face of the God of the Sun, Tonatiuh, appears at the center, surrounded by the symbol for Nahui Ollin (4 Movement). Inside this are the four suns or cosmogonic worlds which had preceded Aztec times, Nahui Ehecatl (4 Wind), Nahui Ocelotl (4 Tiger), Nahui Atl (4 Water), and Nahui Quiahuital (4 Rain of Fire).

"The outside ring shows two great fire-serpents with their tails on one side and their heads with human faces coming from their jaws. . . ."

She stands before the stone, a calendar marking out cycles of twenty-eight days. Here, now, body is registering its own calendar, a minute-by-minute, hour-by-hour plan of a descent again and again into sex that has left her with a strange soreness, half pleasure, half pain. Sex to get beyond sex, is that what this is?

She moves through the large room and enters another where she sees a statue of a dog, its mouth open, its teeth bared, its tongue lolling. But it is not a dog. It is a stone sculpture of a coyote, labeled "Tzintzuntzan, Michoacan."

He is standing behind her, looking at her slimness, at the tilt of her head, at her long neck. He knows she is staring at the stone. There is something so seductive to him in the thought that he can make that staring stop, that he has the power over her to soften that expression. He must get her back to the room, get her back in bed, get to her as he knows he can by now.

He asks if she is ready to go. She says there is more she wants to see.

She turns to a small stone figurine with features of a child, a type referred to as a "baby face." The arms are missing, the mouth open, smiling, not smiling, it is hard to say.

She hurries on to a giant head from Tres Zapotes—

A head without a body—immense, rough, powerful, the stone surface pitted, the eyes unseeing.

There may be no such thing as annihilation in the mind, but maybe there is such a thing as replacement.

After sex in the sweltering afternoon, he lies beside her, sated, his sweating skin next to her sweating skin. But he is aware of a new urgency. It has to do with what is happening now and what has happened to him before, and how these two are severed in him. In the past he has deliberately sought disconnection, cut off others, cut off his previous life as if it had never been. But now he wants her to know who and what he has been, as if it will bind her more closely to him.

He cautions himself not to speak about death, about the deaths he has known, the death of his mother, his father, and the death of his buddy in the war, which should have been his death. Instead he begins to tell her of something that he witnessed. He too is replacing, though he does not think of it as replacing.

As he begins to talk she listens, though she would rather leave things as they have been, in a kind of floating vagueness, transformed into the specific only in the actuality of sex, but she sees he is needing to change that. She herself has no need to tell. She has had enough, too much, of telling, having undergone a process in which telling was the prime focus, requiring memory to give up what it may have never wanted to give, so then why should it not retaliate now by not giving, or if not that, by giving not one answer, but many alternatives, many possibilities, making things up. Take your choice.

Why is he choosing what he is choosing?

They—he is saying—he and the other new recruits—were assembled on the parade ground. Before everyone, one man was to be drummed out of the Corps. They were not told what he had done, they just watched as he was stripped of his insignia, even of his buttons, by the officer in charge. And then he was forced to walk out of the gate to the sound of a single drum beating. It makes him shiver, he says, to think of it, to think how he felt watching. There was terror in him, in everyone, that you could be so cut off, cut off from everybody and everything.

She is thinking that she really doesn't want to hear this. She'd rather let body alone do whatever knowing it can do. Once knowing starts of another kind, the mind's knowing, how images take possession of you, take your eyes prisoner.

There once was a time when she thought you couldn't really

know anyone if you didn't know their history. It was as if they would otherwise float loose, but if you knew their history you could somehow pin them down. But the truth is whatever you know about anyone, they still float loose.

She thinks of saying something to him about this, but then she changes her mind and begins to talk instead of the trip they will take tomorrow.

They had planned to depart early but instead they spend much of the morning in the room, so it is early afternoon before they leave. They drive north on Insurgentes, going past the railroad station, past a Social Security Hospital, and the campus of the Polytechnic Institute. The boulevard is lined with palms on either side. They drive past the turnoff to the Basílica of Guadalupe, past the two statues of Los Indios Verdes, past a picnic area, past a General Electric plant, and a Cafés de Mexico plant, until they come to the town of San Cristóbal Ecatepec. Here they cross a bridge. On each side of the road a dessicated lake bed stretches into the distance.

At seventeen miles from the start, in a village called Venta de Carpio, the road divides. They turn right, pass through the village of San Juan Teotihuacán, and now they see the Pyramids of the Sun and the Moon. They stop at a small government station where they pay two pesos to enter the area, then follow a road to a parking lot near the Pyramid of the Sun.

"The Pyramid of the Sun is 216 feet high, with a base about 750 feet square. It and the smaller Pyramid of the Moon, which is currently being restored, were created long before the Aztecs ruled by a race of

people known only as the predecessors of the Toltecs. It is composed
of five layers of earth and volcanic rock. A tunnel dug into the center of the Pyramid has revealed smaller pyramids within the large
one.

"At the summit, it is now believed, was a huge statue of gold rep-
resenting the God of the Sun."

By the time they start to climb the Pyramid of the Sun, it is midafter-
noon and the sun is very hot. The steps are steep, and in the heat and
the rarefied air the climb begins to feel arduous to her.

He, however, is climbing with what seems like little effort, taking
the steps almost in a bound, as if he is animated by a sudden explosion of energy. There is, she thinks, something in this surefootedness,
in this lightness, that is goatlike.

When they reach the top of the second set of stairs, she says, "You
go on. I'll wait for you here."

"You sure you don't want to—"

"I'm sure," she says.

While he goes farther, she moves to the side to let others go past.
She sits and look out over the countryside, which from this elevation
appears so peaceful and calm. She is no longer inside. Inside grief,
inside rage. There is a certain exaltation in that.

On this massive stone step, on this massive stone monument, people are climbing, passing her.

A haziness comes over her, or is it a haze in the air, a wavering,
from the heat?

As she looks out across the broad plain, something begins in her
eyes, an alteration. The space is altering, the horizon is retreating.
Once again old story, old deception, an old symptom. Once again she

is hostage to eyes, seeing inner events recorded in the outer landscape. As if in sudden self-punishment, what else could it be, revenge for thinking she could escape, has escaped. . . .

Once a hysteric, always a hysteric?

No, she won't believe it.

She turns to look at the tourists, tourists like herself, slowly climbing the stairs, showing evidence of their exertion in the way their chests are heaving, their mouths opening. But among them—climbing among them—this cannot be—yet it is as if it is so—are others, in chains, cruel halters around their necks, dragging them to the temple at the top where they are to be sacrificed, their hearts torn out as offerings to the golden statue of the God of the Sun.

No, of course, she is not seeing this. Her eyes would not deceive her in this way. The harsher part of herself—defender, bypasser, accuser—is stipulating that she is succumbing to the heat, to the altitude, after too much sex, too fast—(What is too much?). A simple return of anxiety—(simple?)—when least expected. An almost willed hallucinating. To prove something.

What could it prove?

Only that in this ancient place, where lives lie in layers, always another life beneath the one above, that events—events that have once taken place—still reverberate—that those who have been still have being. . . .

He has reached the top of the Pyramid. He is pleased with what he has done, pleased with the conquest, having made his way to the top, which few of those climbing have managed to get to. Looking out over the countryside, he is overtaken by excitement. He thinks of her, waiting for him below, sitting on a step. He will stay here only a little longer. He looks out once more upon all that surrounds this Pyramid, small farms, small houses, small hills, and he thinks that back there, back there, far in the distance, is his cabin, a place he holed up in, though now he has no need of such a hideaway.

He starts down the steps. They are rough and uneven, marked by the imprint of feet over many years. A few are passing him on the way to the top. Only one other is descending with him, a young man with a pack on his back, moving rapidly.

When he reaches the top of the second series of steps, where she was waiting, he sees her off to the side, sitting, slumped. He calls her name, and she turns. She looks worn, drained, yet pliant. Pussy-whipped. No. That would be one of Neal's words, not his.

"You should have gone up to the top," he says, "to see the view—" She only nods and smiles. Her face is different from what it was before, not so intense, her eyes, he realizes, not staring in the same way. She is somehow laid open, and he has the sense that he can see right into her, right inside her, see what she is feeling, see what she is thinking.

She is thinking of Edmond, the thought comes to him, as clearly as if someone has shouted it in his ears.

"Let's go down," he says, "let's go back to the car and we can drive over to the Temple of what's-his-name."

"Quetzalcoatl," she says.

"It is believed that a great avenue ran from the Pyramid of the Moon past the Pyramid of the Sun. It was lined by burial chambers for a giant people who all became gods. This Avenue of the Dead led to the Temple of Quetzalcoatl, the Toltec god who ruled as emperor during the Golden Age of the Valley, when the earth was so fertile it

teemed with fruits and flowers, the cotton as it grew took on brilliant hues, and the air was filled with intoxicating perfumes. . . . He
angered the other gods and was forced to flee to the Gulf of Mexico,
where he set sail in a boat made of serpent skin, promising to return
one day. . . ."

On the way back to the city they take the same route they took when
they came but returning, it seems shorter. The farther they are away
from the Pyramids, the more she feels the motion of the car, taking
her away from bumpy roads to the smooth highway, taking her
away from thoughts that are becoming vague as they become more
distant.

Misguided thoughts.

In any case, in the fading light of evening, distant things seem dim.
She's here, in the car, with him. In the real world thoughts, like
events, can be over and done with. Gratefully, she leans back in the
seat and is silent.

He too has become silent. His face is obscured in the onset of
darkness, but now and then it is lit up by the headlights of oncoming cars, which throw into relief a tautness, a rigidity in him. "Is
something the matter?" she asks, after a while.

"Nothing, nothing's the matter."

"You're so quiet."

"We don't have to talk all the time, do we?"

"No," she says. "No, we don't." In fact, they do not talk all that
much, so what does he mean, all the time?

When they get back to the room, he lies on the bed fully clothed, and stares at the ceiling. She asks if he wants to go out to dinner. No, he says, he doesn't want to go out to dinner.

"We've hardly eaten all day."

"I'm not hungry."

"Are you tired?"

He shrugs.

"It's wearing being a tourist," she says.

He turns his head and looks at her. "What makes you say that?"

"I was just thinking how when you're in a strange place—"

He wants to say to her, Admit it, at the Pyramids, you were thinking of him—Edmond—but he can't. If he once says it, the admission of that name into this room will change everything, will ruin everything. But the name is reverberating in his head, as if the name were the person, already present.

He tells himself he has got to stop this. He has got to get this thought out of his head. He puts his thumb and forefinger on the bridge of his nose, and presses tighter and tighter.

"What's the matter?" she asks. "Do you have a headache?"

"No, I don't have a headache."

"Maybe it's the altitude," she says.

"I told you I don't have a headache."

"If you say so."

He shrugs and closes his eyes.

"Maybe it was going to that place. It's such a strange place."

"What place?"

"The Pyramids, of course."

"I didn't see anything strange about them."

"I was only thinking—" She stops and shakes her head. "If I tell you, you'll laugh."

"I won't laugh. Tell me."

As she starts to tell him, she stumbles over the words, trying to recall the thoughts that had seemed so precise and grave to her at the time—about events repeating, going on and on, about the dying, that they keep coming back.

"You were seeing ghosts?"

He laughs, and she laughs, a little.

He grasps her arm. She has been standing close to the bed.

"Any ghost in particular?"

"No, no ghost in particular." She pulls her arm away. "Why are you doing this?"

He is silent for a moment. "Do you always have to know why?"

"Not always."

And she goes into the bathroom and shuts the door.

When she comes out of the bathroom, he is still lying on the bed. She has resolved to get past this, whatever this is. It's crazy to let yourself be sucked into his anxieties. Better to let things go, not to let them build up to the point of explosion.

"Are you sure you don't want something to eat? I could get something light and bring it up here—"

"I'm not hungry. If you're hungry, you go by yourself."

After she has gone, he stares at the ceiling—it has lots of little cracks in the plaster— He has been made a fool of. Even in the sex, yes, even in the sex in this bed, when he was thinking he had this great power over her body, all the time she wasn't even thinking of him.

Yet he was to blame. Didn't he play into it, let himself in for it, being the sucker for this? He almost laughs at his almost joke.

It's not the first time this has happened to him. He has been made a fool of before, he let himself in for it then too, but that was easy to see, much easier to see than what is going on now. He dealt with it. He handled it so it was over with in no time at all. But this isn't like that time.

That time—he hasn't thought of it for so long—it was some years after he and Beryl had been married, she who'd been so honey-voiced telling him how much she loved him, telling him they should get married, and he married her and took her back with him to Clarkstown after the war, and as time went on he began to suspect that she was fucking his best friend Bert, he had no proof at first, but then he found the proof, the absolute proof, she'd had to admit it finally, he'd been right all along, so he left, he left her and left the Midwest—

Thank God, you can take off, thank God, there are escape hatches, that you can drop everything, leave everything behind, leave when you are ready to leave.

Once she is in the coffee shop next door she realizes that, after all, she is not very hungry, either. She orders coffee and some toast, and drinks the coffee but leaves the toast untouched. Maybe, she tells herself, I should just leave tomorrow, change my ticket and go home tomorrow. I don't have to put up with that from him.

After she pays, instead of going up to the room, she goes out into the street. She's been warned about walking in the streets alone at night, but she tells herself she'll be watchful. There's a lot of noise from traffic, the small taxis are darting in and out among the bigger cars and trucks. The sidewalks are crowded with many people going toward the Zócalo. She turns and goes in the opposite direction.

She keeps walking past modern office buildings, until she reaches an area with many small shops. Some are selling silver, some pottery, some a mixture of artifacts. She stops before one window—it has closed by now, as have most of the shops on the street—This shop is called *El Aguila Descalza* and has on its sign a logo of an eagle with bare human feet.

In the window are pieces of black pottery as well as woven material, one of a deep purple with a black border and alternating thin bands of white and black running through it. Next to the material is a little clay figurine, or part of a figurine, that looks as if it once was the top of a container of some kind. It has a circular base that narrows as it rises to the head of a dog. The top part of the dog's face is black, including the eyes and the snout, the rest is unpainted.

As she is looking at the figurine, an older man comes and stands beside her. He is wearing a suit and a tie, and carrying a briefcase. He says something to her in a language that is not Spanish. At the same time he puts out his hand to her, and opens his palm, in which lies a large bill. He looks at her and winks. No, she says, No. She starts to walk away rapidly, turns a corner, then another corner, then another, and looks back. He is not following her.

The street in which she finds herself is dark and very quiet. There is no traffic here. She hurries back the way she came, or thinks it is the way she came, but in fact it takes her to another small street, this one not quite so dark, for there are several dim streetlights along the length of it.

In the doorway of a house that looks abandoned she sees a small boy sleeping. He is curled up against the lintel, his arms wrapped around him. Does he have no home? Even as she is thinking he must be cold, for there is a chill in the air, it is an almost idle thought, for she is still preoccupied, unsure where she is, and, in fact, is fearful, even so, as she stares at the boy, there is a slow leaking, and then a sudden inrush or onrush, a flooding through her, a collapsing of barriers, so she is in that moment in him, lying on that cold cement step, huddled up against the chill of the evening. In that one glimpse he has penetrated into her, made his way into her. It is no longer a matter of just (just?) seeing, as with those figures she saw climbing the Pyramid of the Sun. She is herself and the other.

By the time she reaches the lobby of the hotel she is once again, simply, a tourist, the woman who is staying in room 623. The events in the street are behind her, at a great distance, held off, as if—what is it about this place?—as if here distance can be made large or small at will—

She has decided to take some food up to him in the room, after all, despite what he said.

When she enters the room, she says, "I brought you a ham sandwich, in case you changed your mind, and a beer."

He turns away so she won't see him smile. He feels as if he has won something, but he doesn't want to show it.

She has seen his smile but despite his smile, because of his smile, he looks worn—old and young—and innocent—at the same time—as if he's been pushed beyond endurance by the situation, this bizarre situation between the two of them, free floating and not so free floating, in sex and out of sex. This strange encounter between them that is to go on only a few more days. . . .

With this thought she feels a certain softening, perhaps it is tenderness. Is there in it something of detachment (as if she is standing back, watching him, watching herself)? If it is tenderness, it is also a ruthless acceptance, an acceptance that he and she, in their strangeness to each other in this foreign country, are being acted upon, being brought to some conclusion, not as puppets, for they have will—she could leave at any moment, if she wants to—

It is like a drop, a rise into what is unfinished, unstable, still raw—

And yet it has oddly something of love in it, yes, even in this something of love, and something of repetition: the belief that that which happens can happen again and again, is capable of infinite repetition, as in a story that is told over and over again, and if one teller falters, another takes over. . . .

⌐ 29 ⌐

HE AND SHE ARE DRIVING ON A NARROW COUNTRY ROAD.
On either side are barren stretches of flatland, with here and there
a cultivated field. They have just passed a farm where an animal is
being hitched to a plow.

"It's not a horse?"

"No, a mule."

"I've never seen a mule before."

"Well, you're not a country girl."

"No, I'm not a country girl."

"Mules are much smarter than horses," he says. "If you lead a horse,
the horse will keep on going until it falls over. You can walk him to
death. A mule, it won't keep going. It'll just stop when it's tired."

"The only thing I ever heard about mules was that they were stub-
born, that they stop and don't go when you want them to go—"

"Yeah, but you can get them to move by tricking them. You get behind them, back where they can't see you. And you take two stones and click them together in an irregular pattern."

"Why irregular?"

"If it repeats over and over again, he won't pay attention. So you click them together in an irregular pattern and the mule turns around to see what's going on, and he'll forget why he balked, and he'll just move on."

"That's very interesting," she says. Looking out the window, she sees a lone bird circling overhead, a hawk.

Nothing or very little is being repeated here. Not subjects, not words. But then no one moment of driving is like any other, even if it were the same car—which it is not—even if it were the same road—which it is not—

Just two of them are riding in the old Buick, with blankets, pots, shovels, tools and all sorts of other junk filling the backseat. Together they have been through a brief series of events, in which there has been sex and need and desire, and then, without warning, that whatever it was of his last night, that gloom, that darkness, that was so powerful she had to get out.

Then later, when she came back, he seemed to get over it, or she cajoled him out of it.

God knows, she certainly doesn't want him to be the way he was, stretched out on the bed, silent, angry. It's only that—now that she thinks about it—she feels he came to that change of mood too easily, without effort, just like that. Or rather, she gave in too easily, just like that.

She looks at him, driving. She is making too much of one incident. She's had enough of resentments, transferences, leftover transferences. She was just helping him out. Why shouldn't she? What did she lose by it? At least now he is talking, they are talking, whether of mules or not of mules, whatever they see, what they pass by, just plain talk, talk on the surface, talk creating a surface, talk to be grateful for.

They are on their way to the Villa, where finally, they can spend the night. There was a problem of water, something "overflew," said the manager on the phone, but all that is now taken care of, they are open for guests once again.

As they drive, now and then he hears a warning sound from the engine—a slight rubbing or clicking. When the sound comes, it feels as if it is threatening to dislodge him as much as the car. When it goes, he feels that it was nothing, he's being jumpy for no reason, maybe because of that taco he ate that didn't agree with him, maybe he didn't get enough sleep, though he slept for hours last night.

He sees that she is looking ahead, no, not just looking, staring ahead out of the window. She is thinking—yes, thinking again—thinking of—no, that's over and done with, he's not going to start that again. Things are changing, have changed. The sex last night was different from any other sex they have had. It was almost like they'd been together for years, having had sex for a long long time. . . .

All the different kinds of sex—what Neal said.

A thought comes to him that someday he will look back on this time and will think, At least we had this—we did have this. He has never had such a thought before.

As she drifts between sleeping and waking, falling into sleep, struggling to awake, falling into sleep again, her mind—or whatever part of her mind is taking charge—is trying to arrange a line, a sequence.

It is trying to define what is past, what is over and done with, to give it a history, a shape, and thereby contain it, what followed upon what, what came and what came next, an accounting, a summary: There was driving in the car and there was watching his hands on the wheel, there was being in the cabin in the auto camp, and there was sex with him, it did happen, didn't it, and there was a dog howling, they were at the Pyramids— No, it is wrong, something is wrong, something doesn't belong in here, she'll have to start all over again: There is driving in the car. . . .

If she doesn't get the sequence right, she'll have to start all over again from the beginning. If she can only get it right, it—whatever "it" is—will be solved. (This is no dream, she can feel and hear the movement of the car, she is in a car.)

Glancing over at her, he sees how her body is leaning away from him, her neck stretched taut as her head leans against the window. She groans. He takes his right hand off the wheel and touches her lightly on the shoulder. She opens her eyes, and turns to him, and for an instant she looks startled, as if she does not know who he is.

"You were making a funny noise, kind of groaning," he says. "You must have been dreaming."

"I was having some kind of dream." She shakes her head. "I had to go over and over the same thing, I couldn't get out of it. Do you ever have dreams like that?"

"I almost never dream."

The countryside through which they are passing has begun to change. On either side of the road she sees lush green fields and orchards. They pass through a village, and some children playing in the old plaza wave at them. She waves back, and they wave again and call out some words she does not understand.

Beyond the village the road widens and is smoothly paved.

"How long will it take us to get there?" she asks him.

"It depends on the road. If it's like this, three hours. If not, maybe four or five, longer."

"It will be dark."

"Yes."

Simple, direct words.

She is wondering what the Villa will be like in the dark. A dark place without a harsh word, a dark place where she will find an ending, happy or not, happy just because it will be an ending.

"Maybe we will get there before dark," she says.

"We might."

The Villa is situated at the farthest end of town, near the river. They get out of the car and walk through a gate that opens onto a lush tropical garden filled with exotic flowers. A huge tree stands at the center of the garden. In the dim light—it is almost but not quite dark—it is hard to make out the color of the blossoms.

A man comes out of one of the thatched huts surrounding the garden. He says he is the manager, greets them by name, and apologizes for the delay. "But now everything is good. I'll show you to your little house. You will be very comfortable here."

It is a one-room hut with a palm-thatched roof, plaster walls, and a cement floor. The showers and toilet are in the next building. There is no electricity yet, he explains, but there is a kerosene lamp, which he will light for them. Vern says not to bother, he can do it, but the manager insists on lighting the lamp anyhow. "Our dining room is at the opposite, across the garden. We are serving the dinner now," he says and leaves.

She looks around the room, which is sparsely furnished. Beside the bed there are several straight chairs, a wooden trestle table, a wooden hook to hang clothes on, and a small carved wooden chest. The walls are white. The bed has no spread but is made up with fresh linen, smelling as if it's been dried in sunlight.

In the dining room—or dining hut—they are served margaritas. This hut also has a thatched roof, but is open to the air on three sides. Only two other people are dining, a man and a woman, an older couple, who for the most part eat silently.

He has asked the manager if Lila is around but the manager said she is still in the States. He thinks of her in that house in Sunnyvale with the desertlike front yard and the little shepherds and shepherdesses inside that he never noticed, that house where Neal told his story, a story that was, what did he say, true enough.

"Want another drink?"

"No, I'll stick with this one."

He orders another margarita for himself, he's had more than two, he's not counting. Something about this place is making him uneasy, irritable. He tries to tell himself it's only for two days. It was his idea, after all, to come here, no matter what Neal said about it.

She sips her drink. "It's so nice here."

"What were you expecting?"

"I thought it would be primitive, I never expected it to be so nice."

"I've noticed something about you," he says.

"Oh?"

"I've noticed you usually expect the worst." His voice is edgy, suggestive, though he's still smiling.

How does he come up with that "usually," after knowing her for such a short time? Whatever he's doing, it's one of his moods, don't let him get to you. "Well, maybe, sometimes." She laughs. "It's my Golden Rule: the less you expect the better off you are."

"Oh? So you won't be disappointed?"

"I guess. Maybe. No matter what happens, no matter what anyone does—"

"It looks to me like you're asking for a lot of unnecessary misery." Then he adds, "Do you like misery?"

"No, no, of course not."

"So then, what is it?"

"I look at it this way." She's not sure which way she looks at it, but the effect of the margaritas compels her to go on. "If you're going to be disappointed, okay, I mean, everybody gets disappointed, but at least you've prepared yourself for it."

"And that makes it easier."

"I think so."

"What if it turns out to be better than what you thought?"

"Then you're that much ahead."

"Ahead, how?"

"Maybe if you believe it is going to be worse, that helps ensure it's going to be better."

"I don't get it."

"Maybe it helps appease the gods," she says and laughs.

Because of this place and the margaritas, everything is easier, everything is slowed down. Even the night air seems soft and slow, heavy with the scent of the exotic flowers.

She looks at the older couple: they are still silent. When you've been together for so long, she thinks, you probably don't even need to talk, you probably know each other's thoughts.

"Never a harsh word," she says.

He is stretched out on the bed. He is staring at the thatched roof. He knows he has had too much to drink. When it happened when he was with the girl in Big Sur, everything got hazy. Now everything is achingly clear, stripping the falseness from this false paradise. All she was saying at dinner, in that conversation at dinner, was a con. She was pretending, or mocking him in some way, being superior in her knowing way, judging him and finding him wanting.

"What gods?" he asks her.

"What are you talking about?"

"Appeasing what gods?"

"Oh," she says, "any gods, all gods." She picks up her toiletry case and goes out the door.

He lies there in wait, not knowing what he is waiting for, except that he wants these thoughts to go away. He puts his thumb and forefinger on either side of the bridge of his nose, and presses hard. The thoughts go away but new thoughts rush in to take their place. He sits up and looks around the room, and his eyes light on the kerosene lamp that the manager insisted on lighting, as if he was incapable of doing it himself.

When she comes back in, he asks her, "Do you think he was a good man?"

"Who are you talking about?" she asks. She knows who he is talking about.

"Edmond, was he a good man?"

It is true that when he first saw Edmond, he had this feeling of excitement, that he had met somebody who was like somebody's idea of a hero, no, that he was like his own idea of a hero, the way he looked, the way he talked . . . and even more than that, he had a way of making you feel you could trust him, that no matter what, you could trust him. When he said he wanted to go gold panning or hunting, it made you feel special that this man wanted to go with you, wanted to spend time with you. But then, when he called him he had been too busy. That's what he'd said.

She looks and him and sighs. "It's hard to say about anybody, if they're good or not."

"Why do you say that?"

"It's just that it's hard to know." She shrugs.

The gesture enrages him, as if she is shrugging him off.

"But you think you're good, don't you?"

"Why do you say that?" She flushes. "No, I don't. The good people I know, I'm not like them, unselfish, always thinking of the other person. No, I'm not like that."

He persists. "But was he a good man or not?"

"Why do you keep harping on him?"

Why? He's dead, and yet here in this hut with the damn smell of those tropical flowers practically smothering him, the thought of him is alive, even if he wanted to get rid of the thought of him, he can't or won't.

"Come on, you can tell me."

"I told you, it's hard to say."

The madness in this is that the more she won't talk about him, the more he is driven to ask about him, to know for certain all there is to know about him and her. Yet he doesn't want to do this. He should stop pushing at her. Even if she is lying. And surely she is lying. But he can't stop it. "I'm only bringing him up because I know what you're thinking. I can see it in your face, in your eyes."

"Why are you doing this? It's not like you, acting this way."

"Not like me? What am I like?" His voice is harsh in his throat, and yet he can feel himself grinning. "If you're so smart, what am I like?"

She closes her eyes. Then she lets out her breath, loudly, and turns away.

"No? Then you want me to tell you what I'm like? Sure, I'll tell you. I've got stories, lots of stories for you."

"But—" she says.

But he has gotten up from the bed, he is walking back and forth in the room, pacing, he has already begun to tell.

He is telling about how he met Beryl during the war, when he was at El Toro. She was a bit player in the movies. She was small, slim, blonde. She wouldn't sleep with him, she said, until he married her, though he later found out she'd already slept with some of the other guys, God knows how many. He had a fear at the time, not because of the war, that he might get killed—he really didn't ever think he would get killed—but because he knew he was out of control, doing anything and everything wild that anybody suggested. Being married, he figured, would get him back in control. The only thing, he insisted, she had to convert to Catholicism. He himself hadn't practiced for a long time, but these were his terms.

When he came back after the war, they went to live in Clarkstown, where he'd lived as a kid. His family was there. He went to school on the G.I. Bill. Later he got a job at the bank. He was working all day, she wasn't. She wanted to go out every night, he'd say okay. She'd want to go out to dinner, and to a club. They'd go with Jill and Bert Logan, Bert was his best friend. The four of them were always together. Little by little, it was one of those things that dawns on you, a little hint here, a little hint there, he began to realize that she was fucking Bert, but he had no way of proving it. He even asked her. She said, Of course not. Still, he knew. So he decided, what's sauce for the goose is sauce for the gander, and he started screwing around too. There were lots of women, all willing.

Then one day a woman came into the bank to ask for a loan. This woman was a real good friend of Beryl's best friend, and he figured she could find out, she could get him the dirt on Beryl. So he asked her out, and had sex with her, and even said he loved her and wanted to marry her, but to marry her he'd have to divorce Beryl, and to divorce Beryl he had to have evidence, and that wasn't so easy, so he asked her to find out what she could about Beryl from Beryl's best friend.

She found out, gave him chapter and verse, about when and where Beryl was meeting Bert.

So now he had the goods on her, but he waited a while, he had to do it at the right moment. One night they weren't going out, they brought in hamburgers—she never cooked—and the telephone rang, and he answered it. It was somebody asking for donations to the Knights of Columbus. When he hung up, she said, Who was that? He said, It was an anonymous call. He said, Somebody said you're having an affair with Bert. And of course, she got mad and denied it. So then he started reeling off all the facts, saying, What about this time? What about this place? And she turned pale. She admitted it, she broke down and admitted it all, but she said, I really love you, I always loved you. She didn't know he was recording every word she was saying, so he'd have the evidence against her for the divorce.

The next thing she's gone into the bedroom and shut the door, and he can hear her crying, but he's not listening, and the next thing after that, he's hearing a loud noise, it's a gunshot, and he runs into the bedroom, and finds her weeping, waving the gun.

He grabbed the gun and said, What the hell do you think you're doing? I want to kill myself, she said. Oh sure, that's why you shot at the wall, is it? One more lie, trying to make me feel sorry for you. Well, I'm not going to feel sorry for you. I want you out of this house, now.

So she got out, went to Cleveland, where she had a sister. But she came back, six months later. Fuck off, he told her. She said, Not me. This time I'm not leaving, you're leaving. You're dreaming, girl, he told her. She said, If you don't, I'll tell your mother that for all these years, you were pretending, telling her you were going to Mass on Sunday in another church in town, when you were driving out of town with your buddies—

"All of a sudden, I didn't care. It wasn't even what she was going to tell my mother, I didn't give a damn finally about that. I knew that everything there was over for me, not just my life with her, but my life in the town. All those years—she was doing me a favor, though she didn't know it.

"So I said, 'Give me two days, and I'll be gone.'"

She has been looking at him. All the time he has been talking and pacing, she has been wondering, Is this what he is like, this man I thought was so bland, hiding behind his blandness? Now, in the cold light of the kerosene lamp, the blandness is gone and he is someone capable of planning, of plotting, of taping, and yet, at the end, he gives it all up.

Mournful, she looks mournful to him. He thinks he even sees a tear in her eye. But he is in no mood to allow himself to be touched by her tears.

"Why is it that when someone tells you something, you act like it happened to you?"

"That's not what I was doing. I was just thinking maybe Beryl did mean to kill herself, but the gun didn't go off right."

"It's always your own story you've got to be making up. Do yourself a favor," he says. "Stop with the goddam thinking."

"How am I going to do that?"

Pay attention to me, he thinks, pay attention to me, in sex, and out of sex. But it is a thought so filled with rage and shame that it cannot be said, it must take an underground path from him to her.

"What was he to you? You and he, how did you get together?"

"What does it matter?

"I'd just like to know."

She is silent.

"So don't tell, that's okay with me."

And once again, he is pacing, he is telling.

He is telling what happened when he went to visit his sister Peg, who was almost twenty years older than him. It was soon after he told Beryl to get out, and he was feeling like he was free again, a little out of control, he was taking pleasure in that feeling. So he drove down to see Peg in Abbotsville, a small town in the southern part of the state.

Peg's husband, Andy, was a quiet guy, who had a business in auto parts. He wasn't much in evidence, he was always working, or when he wasn't working, he was in the garage, playing with his model railroad trains. Peg was the one who ran the house, ran him. She was a big woman who made her opinions known loudly. As her youngest brother, he'd always been her favorite. She was happy to have him come visit, glad to have him stay as long as he liked, blamed Beryl for all that had happened, called her that little bitch. It was nice to have someone on your side.

Peg and Andy had three daughters, one sixteen, one seventeen and one eighteen, each one better looking than the next. From the minute he came, they flirted with him. Well, more than flirted. The oldest one, Sally, gave him a big wet kiss on the mouth when he arrived.

He was staying in the downstairs rec room, which had a big bed in it, and a TV set. Early one morning, it was still dark, Sally came in and got into bed with him. At first it was just cuddling, then it started getting hotter, she was anxious for it, he could tell, and soon he was fucking her. It got to be a nice morning habit. And then one day she came in and it was still dark, they started at it, but she was different this time, she was tighter, he had a hard time getting into her, and then when it was light, he saw it wasn't Sally, it was June, the middle one, she'd come in wearing the same wrapper Sally always wore. June said it was her first time. He said, Why didn't you tell me it was your first time? Then the next morning, he was waiting and wondering, would it be Sally or June, but this time it was neither one of them, it was Andrea, the youngest, she slipped in in the same wrapper, and the first thing, before anything else happened, she was going down on him.

She is looking at him now, he can see her looking at him, trying to make him out. Let her try. He feels a little like a performer, playing a part, someone not giving a damn—like Neal—more like Neal is—though she doesn't know Neal— As if the more he can make himself like Neal, the easier he can break something in her, that pity in her, that bleeding heart in her.

"But your sister, Peg, did she know, what did she think of what was going on?"

"What did she think about my balling her three daughters? Well, I'll tell you, I think she knew, I think she even got a certain pleasure from it." Was this so? It could have been so. He wouldn't be surprised if it was so.

Was that what Peg was getting out of it, some kind of satisfaction from that mutual fantasy in a rec room in an ordinary house in an ordinary town, where everybody was expected to act in a certain way, but not in this way?

She feels as if she's been struck by lightning and she's fallen on the ground—what was that play she once saw in which a blind man falls and when he gets up, he can see?—and she's picked herself up from the ground, only to realize that she's okay, still alive, but she's been seeing things wrong, been seeing everything through a veil. She's been shut up inside her head, inside her body, clinging like a drowning woman to all that passion and denial of passion—and guilt.

And all the time in everyday life, out there, this one is screwing that one, uncle, niece, whatever. And where's the guilt? No guilt. What a fool I am. How naïve I have been, and unknowing for all my thinking I was solving anything through thinking.

"I was his patient," she says. "I was Edmond's patient."

"His patient, no kidding. The guy who was supposed to make you better from whatever was wrong with you, he fucked you?" When she does not respond, he goes on. "I have this friend who says there are so many different kinds of sex you can't begin to count them. So what was this one like?" he asks. "Sort of like fucking a priest?" His lips widen to a grin. "What did you do?"

"Do?"

"What did he do? What did you do?"

She won't say. She can't say. Say what? That there was this touch, then that touch, this movement, then that movement, this sound, that sound. . . .

It happened.

Suddenly he looks deflated, as if his whole body is on the verge of collapse. As if he has fallen into absolute fatigue, or grief.

"Jesus," he says. "I've got to stop this. This is killing me. You're killing me."

He goes over to the bed and falls on it, fully clothed. Instantly, he is asleep.

CHAPTER

↶ 30 ↷

IS THIS THE ENDING SHE HAS BEEN GOING TOWARD? TO LIE in bed next to him, he in a dead sleep, having said this is killing him? She is killing him. The kerosene lamp still lights the room with its cold glow. She does not know how to turn it off. She is detecting a familiar smell, of alcohol coming off of skin. (But outside there is no dog howling.)

To lie next to another. To hear another's breath. To see him closed off, contained in his sleep. At least in sleep, unchanging.

She has come here, thinking it was a way out. Instead, she has ended up inside, inside a room, lying next to a man of only seeming diffidence and silence, capable of weird jealousies, and sudden out-bursts, designed to force her to abandon her idea of him.

What does it mean to have an idea of someone? Does it mean that no matter what he says, what he does, what he tells, and doesn't tell, he is still one and the same being, you don't have to keep revising? As if by making him one, you can make yourself one?

He has accused her of taking others' stories and appropriating them as her own, weeping for herself, not for them. It is not true. It is not quite true. It is only that she finds her life in their life. In an instant of listening, the place where they have their being becomes the place she has being, even though she knows it isn't really so.

She has become—she always was—incomplete, waiting for the stories of those outside to complete her.

Outside, yes, there is an outside.

The smell of the flowers is thick in the room. Outside this thatched hut is the garden with the large tree and all the other huts. In one hut the old couple lies asleep, one tightly clasping the other, a pair of spoons nestling.

Outside the gate is the town, shuttered now, quiet. Chickens quiet, goats quiet, mules quiet. In a white house with a tiled roof, a woman is nursing a child. She lifts the child to her shoulder and pats it on the back. Then she puts the child in a cradle and rocks the cradle, gently. Not harshly.

(Julie is so far away, with Michael and Edith. How she wishes she could see her, hold her.)

"Goddammit!" he yells.

"Get away from me! A fucking mosquito is biting me!" He has jumped out of bed and is flailing at the air.

She gets up and stands before him, trying to wake him, to calm him. "Take it easy, Vern."

He brushes her aside. "Get out of my way, girl." He is another man, with another voice, another expression on his face, his eyes staring but not seeing. Girl, he is calling her girl. He doesn't even know who she is.

"I'm getting out of here. Where are my keys?"

He looks around wildly. She sees them on the table. She moves so as to get the table between her and him, so he won't see them. She gathers them up in her left hand behind her back. He should not drive in the state he is in.

"Where the fuck did I put them? I know I put them down somewhere. So where are they?"

"You can look for them in the morning. Why don't you go back to bed now?"

He is muttering, "I know I put them down here—somewhere."

"In the morning you'll be able to see better."

"I can see all I need to see." He turns quickly, stumbles and almost falls. She puts out her right hand to steady him.

"Don't touch me!" He shoves her hand away. "Don't try to stop me. Nobody's going to stop me. I'm going to get my car. I know where my car is. I know where I left it."

He opens the door and steps out into the garden.

"Vern, how are you going to drive without your keys?"

"Just leave me be, girl. I have my secrets. If you want to know, I've got a key right under the right fender."

She goes out after him. "Here," she says, "I have your keys. Maybe you should let me come with you, maybe you should let me drive."

He reaches out, and takes the keys from her hand.

"I am going solo."

She sits on the edge of the bed, her hands on her knees. It is a rigid posture that keeps her in place, that holds her upright. But she cannot stop trembling.

He could kill himself, driving on those roads. She should have stopped him, she tried to stop him, she should have tried to ask for help. No, he wanted to go. She had to let him go. She should have awakened the manager. What could he have done? He would not have interfered. A man wants to drive. You let him drive. Is the trembling getting worse? The trembling is getting worse. She cannot contain it. She cannot stop it. She is shaking so hard, it is as if some outside force is shaking her.

He will probably come back. It is her mind telling her this, while her body is dictating, breeding terror within her.

How did she get herself into this? It's her own fault, her own fault. She tries to lay out all the reasons why this has happened and has happened before. Is he going to come back? He will probably come back. He may not come back. Is he going to come back? She has come back to where she began, no rules, order, sequence— no near, no far, no now, no then, only the continual splitting of anxiety.

With his headlights on high, he has been driving over rough roads, narrow roads, roads that lead to nowhere. He has been forced to turn back and back again.

At least he is going—he is getting out—there's not a fucking thing to stop him—he is on this road—a dark road—his headlights lighting it up—no cliffs on either side—just going—leaving it all behind— they tried their damnedest to stop him, taking away his keys—let them try—they tried to make out that he is a fool—fuck them all— he doesn't need them—just keep on going from this place—he doesn't need to know what place—as long as he's left it all behind—as long as he's not the one left behind—

Yet all the time, for all his rage, he is careful, he is not a fool, he is driving carefully, careful not to take chances, that's the point, not to take chances, always watch your back— No, there's no one behind him—he is checking the rear view mirror—no one is following him—that's for sure—finally he is free of the ones who want nothing but to tear him down—

He's showed them his butt—

He starts to laugh but the laugh catches in his throat—it could just as well be a sob—what the hell—as if he were a kid—a goddam kid— he swallows—all that he's been forced to swallow—like when he said to Neal, I'd sure like to come, and Neal said, Your idea of fun is not my idea of fun, Your thing is not— Like when he invited Edmond to come gold panning and Edmond said, Don't call me, I'll call you.

Fuck them, just fuck them all.

The kerosene lamp has gone out by itself, sputtered and left a stinging smell in the air, entangled with the scent of the flowers. She is stiff, she is cold. She has wrapped herself in a blanket from the bed, but she is still shivering.

Outside, there is violence in the night—outside the gate— In a bar at the center of town, a bar filled with loud music and a lot of noise, a fight has started between two men, whose voices get louder and louder, until they rush outside to fight, and one pulls out a knife—and blood is streaming, the life of one leaking out. . . .

In the moonlight, a shadow is moving on the white wall. He has come in, silently. He pays her no heed. He is packing up his things. She can say or do nothing. She can only sit and watch, she is paralyzed watching him leave. Yet she is in his mind as he leaves, looking back and seeing her silent figure, sitting on the bed.

She awakens. It is morning. He has not come back yet. If he doesn't come, she will have to make her way to Mexico City by bus, if there is a bus, or get a ride somehow.

It is midmorning by the time he drives up to the gate of the Villa.

He parks and walks through the garden to the hut and opens the door. She is not there, though her case is packed. He stands there, uncertain. He is grimy, his hands black, his left hand is burned, not badly, but burned.

How did that happen?

It comes back to him like a dream, vaguely. Ahead, in the road, is a strange light, small at first then getting larger as he approaches. It is a fire. It is a wreck. Two cars have collided at an intersection, and one of them is engulfed in flame. He stops, he sees a man trying to pull someone from the burning car, he jumps out of the Buick and opens the rear door, pulls out one blanket, two, runs to the car, throws the blankets over the man being pulled from the car, he is still alive, moaning—the other man is shouting "*El doctor!*" is shouting "*Clínica! El doctor!*" —is pointing down the dark road, "*Clínica!*"

Then—what? He took the man, he took the two men, in the backseat of the Buick. . . .

No, it was not a dream. He is grimy, his hand is burned. If he could only find some ointment. Perhaps she has some ointment. He is remembering the ointment his mother used on them when they were kids, when they got burned. Mrs. Buffington's Drawing Salve.

He goes to see the manager. He asks him if he has some salve. The manager looks at his hand. The best thing, he says, I have the best thing. He brings him back a fruit from a small tree in the garden. He squeezes the pulp from the fruit, and puts it on the burn. No, he says, no bandage, it must be open to the air.

He goes back to the hut, he cannot stay here. He feels revulsion in this hut, against this hut. He goes next door to take a shower. The water pressure is so low it's like a trickle, the cross-section of the pipe must be about the size of a needle. But at least the water is cold and soothing as it drips down his skin. He is thinking of the baths in Big Sur. He is feeling things wash out of him.

After breakfast, she has walked through the garden, noticed the pur-ple blossoms on the large tree, inspected the many orchids, the white outer leaves, lightly striped with pink, the sheltered inner leaves, a deeper pink, has gone out the gate, has walked along a country lane past haciendas, small ones with gardens, and has made her way down to the river. There she has stopped to watch two women on the bank washing clothes, watched the dipping of the clothes in the water, the beating of the clothes on the rocks, the laying out of the clothes on the rocks in the sun. She has walked farther, has seen a sandbar jut-ting into the river and now she has gone out onto the sandbar.

Across the river, on the other side, is a landscape different from this side, a hillside covered with dry brush, more brown than green, look-ing eroded, studded with cacti, split by a lateral path, like a slash in the brush, winding through the brush. She has noted all this, as if she is storing up information for a later time.

Where is the waterfall? Didn't he say something about a waterfall?

She has come back to the room. She has seen his keys on the dresser. He has been here but he is not here. She sits on a chair by the win-dow. The sun is streaming through the window onto her back. She does not move away from its warmth. She sits and waits.

His head down, he comes in hesitantly. He is like the old Vern, the first time she saw him. He comes in without seeing her and then he turns slowly, as if trying to decide something. When he sees her, he lets out a startled sound.

"What's the matter?"

"I—I—I thought—for a minute—the way the sun was behind you—the way your face was in shadow—I thought you were a nun."

"A nun?"

He is not going to tell her about Maggie (he is through with telling), about his twin sister Maggie who became a nun, who went into an order in Kansas, they all thought she was set for life. But then, one day the Mother Superior called. Maggie had disappeared, she'd been gone for four days. Gone over the wall. The Mother Superior didn't say that, but that was what she had done. When he went down to the convent, they took him into a room. The Mother Superior and two other nuns were sitting behind a table. Behind them was a big window, and the sun was shining through the window so he was almost blinded, he couldn't see their faces, just their black outlines. The Mother Superior said Maggie had run away with a priest. She said he should talk to her, she said maybe he could persuade her to come back. Of course, he didn't even try. He didn't say no, but he didn't try. He didn't hear from Maggie until just after his divorce. She called him. She and the priest were married. They started having kids right away. She said she'd gained a lot of weight.

He moves over to the bed. He sits on the edge of the bed. From this angle he can see her face. "Why are you smiling?"

"Because you thought I was a nun. You know, Vern, I'm a Jew."

"No, I didn't know. How would I know?"

She is thinking of all the things she could tell him about herself beside the fact that she is a Jew: where she was born, who her mother and father were, where she went to school—and maybe about the time when she was eighteen or nineteen and she and her lover, David, had just parted, and she went with a girlfriend to a seaside resort. They found the resort almost deserted—it was during the war—but two sailors on leave came by for the day, and they picked them up, and in the heat of the day she slept with one of them. She did not know why she did this. She was still in love with David, she still hoped to get back with him. With the sailor it was oddly impersonal on her part, as if it was an offering of some kind—to this man, that man, any man.

"Are you religious?" he asks.

"No, I'm not religious. What difference does it make?"

"No difference."

She shrugs.

He stands up. "I see you're packed. It'll take me a minute to get my stuff together."

She is silent, watching him. When he is done, he says, "If you're ready, we can go now."

She is still sitting. "Before we go," she asks, "can we sit for a minute?"

"I have nothing more to say." he says. He wants her to say to him that there is no other, no other for her but him, only he knows that she will never say that, and maybe it is just as well that she will never say that. Still he stands and waits.

And she, in the silence, she is sitting, she is waiting, is it to tell him something or not?

He is not looking at her. He has turned away from her, a baffled, innocent, desperate look on his face. I am not good for him, she thinks. No wonder he had to leave. No wonder he said, Don't touch me. As Julie said, Don't touch me.

I would turn away from myself if I could, from this constant thinking that goes nowhere, from this anxiety that is the one absolute I can always count on. I would turn away if I could from this desperate need to fall into the unknown—it is and maybe it always was an addiction to me, even when I had no name for it, still I needed it, wanted it, and will I always need it and want it and fear it?

"Are you ready? Can we go now?"

"Please, not yet Vern. Just a moment longer."

"What good do you think this is doing?"

Maybe I am looking for a better ending—for you, and for me. So that afterward, when we look back, it will not be with shame or regret, she is about to say. But what good will it do to say that to him? Maybe more harm than good.

I have said these words before. They were not right then, they are not right now.

He picks up one case and starts to get another. She notices that he winces as he lifts the second case.

"Are you all right?" she asks.

"I'm all right."

"Well—" he says, and goes out.

She stands and looks around the room before she goes out the door. She will never see this room again. She looks at the bed, at the chest, at the white walls, at the wooden hook. She looks at each thing, as if it might provide her with an answer, or at least tell her something about which there can be no argument. That someday there may be other rooms for other kinds of telling, about which there will be certainty or perhaps even truth, rooms waiting to be resided in. . . .

After he puts the cases in the trunk, she is about to get into the car beside him, but first she looks into the backseat. It is completely empty. What has happened to everything that was there? she is about to ask him, but then decides not to.

"I smell something burning," she says.

"Nothing is burning now."

ABOUT THE AUTHOR

After first receiving her undergraduate degree in physics from Hunter College and serving as a junior physicist at the Palmer Physical Laboratory at Princeton University at the end of World War II (in addition to a later stint at Oak Ridge), Millicent Dillon has gone on to have one of the most distinguished careers in American arts and letters. A novelist, a biographer and a playwright, Dillon has received a fellowship from the Guggenheim Foundation and three grants from the National Endowment for the Humanities.

Five times the recipient of O. Henry Awards for short stories, Dillon was also a finalist for the PEN/Faulkner Award for Fiction in 2001 for her last novel, *Harry Gold*, which was named a *New York Times* Notable Book. Her short stories, essays and reviews have appeared in *Southwest Review, Threepenny Review, The Nation, The Times Literary Supplement,* and *The New Yorker,* among other publications, and her previous works of fiction are *The Dance of the Mothers, The One in the Back Is Medea,* and her debut work, *Baby Perpetua and Other Stories.* A widely respected authority on the lives of Paul Bowles and Jane Bowles, Dillon is the author of *A Little Original Sin: The Life and Works of Jane Bowles* and *You Are Not I: A Portrait of Paul Bowles,* and has edited *Out in the World: The Selected Letters of Jane Bowles* and *The Viking Portable Paul and Jane Bowles.* She has also written a widely praised dual biography of Isadora Duncan and Mary Cassatt.

The author of four plays, *She Is in Tangier, Prisoners of Ordinary Need, By the Water,* and *Inside,* the last two commissioned by Bay Area Radio Drama. Dillon, who was a resident of the Bay Area for half a century, now lives in Tallahassee, Florida.